FANTASTIC FABLES

by
Ambrose
Bierce

DOVER PUBLICATIONS, INC.
NEW YORK

Published in Canada by General Publishing Company, Ltd., 30 Lesmill Road, Don Mills, Toronto, Ontario.

Published in the United Kingdom by Constable and Company, Ltd., 10 Orange Street, London WC2.

This Dover edition, first published in 1970, is an unabridged republication of the work originally published by G. P. Putnam's Sons, New York, in 1898.

Standard Book Number: 486-22225-X
Library of Congress Catalog Card Number: 73-92026

Manufactured in the United States of America
Dover Publications, Inc.
180 Varick Street
New York, N.Y. 10014

CONTENTS

The Fables

Aesopus Emendatus

Old Saws with New Teeth

THE FABLES

The Moral Principle and
the Material Interest

A Moral Principle met a Material Interest on a bridge
wide enough for but one.

"Down, you base thing!" thundered the Moral Principle,
"and let me pass over you!"

The Material Interest merely looked in the other's eyes
without saying anything.

"Ah," said the Moral Principle, hesitatingly, "let us draw
lots to see which shall retire till the other has crossed."

The Material Interest maintained an unbroken silence and
an unwavering stare.

"In order to avoid a conflict," the Moral Principle resumed, somewhat uneasily, "I shall myself lie down and let
you walk over me."

Then the Material Interest found a tongue, and by a
strange coincidence it was its own tongue. "I don't think you
are very good walking," it said. "I am a little particular
about what I have underfoot. Suppose you get off into the
water."

It occurred that way.

The Crimson Candle

A man lying at the point of death called his wife to his bedside and said:

"I am about to leave you forever; give me, therefore, one
last proof of your affection and fidelity, for, according to our
holy religion, a married man seeking admittance at the gate
of Heaven is required to swear that he has never defiled himself with an unworthy woman. In my desk you will find a
crimson candle, which has been blessed by the High Priest

and has a peculiar mystical significance. Swear to me that while it is in existence you will not remarry."

The Woman swore and the Man died. At the funeral the Woman stood at the head of the bier, holding a lighted crimson candle till it was wasted entirely away.

The Blotted Escutcheon
and the Soiled Ermine

A Blotted Escutcheon, rising to a question of privilege, said:

"Mr. Speaker, I wish to hurl back an allegation and explain that the spots upon me are the natural markings of one who is a direct descendant of the sun and a spotted fawn. They come of no accident of character, but inhere in the divine order and constitution of things."

When the Blotted Escutcheon had resumed his seat a Soiled Ermine rose and said:

"Mr. Speaker, I have heard with profound attention and entire approval the explanation of the honourable member, and wish to offer a few remarks on my own behalf. I, too, have been foully calumniated by our ancient enemy, the Infamous Falsehood, and I wish to point out that I am made of the fur of the *Mustela maculata*, which is dirty from birth."

The Ingenious Patriot

Having obtained an audience of the King an Ingenious Patriot pulled a paper from his pocket, saying:

"May it please your Majesty, I have here a formula for constructing armour-plating which no gun can pierce. If these plates are adopted in the Royal Navy our warships will be invulnerable, and therefore invincible. Here, also, are reports of your Majesty's Ministers, attesting the value of the invention. I will part with my right in it for a million tumtums."

After examining the papers, the King put them away and promised him an order on the Lord High Treasurer of the Extortion Department for a million tumtums.

"And here," said the Ingenious Patriot, pulling another paper from another pocket, "are the working plans of a gun that I have invented, which will pierce that armour. Your Majesty's Royal Brother, the Emperor of Bang, is anxious to purchase it, but loyalty to your Majesty's throne and person constrains me to offer it first to your Majesty. The price is one million tumtums."

Having received the promise of another check, he thrust his hand into still another pocket, remarking:

"The price of the irresistible gun would have been much greater, your Majesty, but for the fact that its missiles can be so effectively averted by my peculiar method of treating the armour plates with a new——"

The King signed to the Great Head Factotum to approach.

"Search this man," he said, "and report how many pockets he has."

"Forty-three, Sire," said the Great Head Factotum, completing the scrutiny.

"May it please your Majesty," cried the Ingenious Patriot, in terror, "one of them contains tobacco."

"Hold him up by the ankles and shake him," said the King; "then give him a check for forty-two million tumtums and put him to death. Let a decree issue declaring ingenuity a capital offence."

Two Kings

The King of Madagao, being engaged in a dispute with the King of Bornegascar, wrote him as follows:

"Before proceeding further in this matter I demand the recall of your Minister from my capital."

Greatly enraged by this impossible demand, the King of Bornegascar replied:

"I shall not recall my Minister. Moreover, if you do not immediately retract your demand I shall withdraw him!"

This threat so terrified the King of Madagao that in hastening to comply he fell over his own feet, breaking the Third Commandment.

An Officer and a Thug

A Chief of Police who had seen an Officer beating a Thug was very indignant, and said he must not do so any more on pain of dismissal.

"Don't be too hard on me," said the Officer, smiling; "I was beating him with a stuffed club."

"Nevertheless," persisted the Chief of Police, "it was a liberty that must have been very disagreeable, though it may not have hurt. Please do not repeat it."

"But," said the Officer, still smiling, "it was a stuffed Thug."

In attempting to express his gratification, the Chief of Police thrust out his right hand with such violence that his skin was ruptured at the arm-pit and a stream of sawdust poured from the wound. He was a stuffed Chief of Police.

The Conscientious Official

While a Division Superintendent of a railway was attending closely to his business of placing obstructions on the track and tampering with the switches he received word that the President of the road was about to discharge him for incompetency.

"Good Heavens!" he cried; "there are more accidents on my division than on all the rest of the line."

"The President is very particular," said the Man who brought him the news; "he thinks the same loss of life might be effected with less damage to the company's property."

"Does he expect me to shoot passengers through the car windows?" exclaimed the indignant official, spiking a loose tie across the rails. "Does he take me for an assassin?"

How Leisure Came

A Man to Whom Time Was Money, and who was bolting his breakfast in order to catch a train, had leaned his newspaper against the sugar-bowl and was reading as he ate. In his haste and abstraction he stuck a pickle-fork into his right eye, and on removing the fork the eye came with it. In buying spectacles the needless outlay for the right lens soon reduced him to poverty, and the Man to Whom Time Was Money had to sustain life by fishing from the end of a wharf.

The Moral Sentiment

A Pugilist met the Moral Sentiment of the Community, who was carrying a hat-box. "What have you in the hat-box, my friend?" inquired the Pugilist.

"A new frown," was the answer. "I am bringing it from the frownery—the one over there with the gilded steeple."

"And what are you going to do with the nice new frown?" the Pugilist asked.

"Put down pugilism—if I have to wear it night and day," said the Moral Sentiment of the Community, sternly.

"That's right," said the Pugilist, "that is right, my good friend; if pugilism had been put down yesterday, I wouldn't have this kind of Nose to-day. I had a rattling hot fight last evening with——"

"Is that so?" cried the Moral Sentiment of the Community, with sudden animation. "Which licked? Sit down here on the hat-box and tell me all about it!"

The Politicians

An Old Politician and a Young Politician were travelling through a beautiful country, by the dusty highway which leads to the City of Prosperous Obscurity. Lured by the flowers and the shade and charmed by the songs of birds which invited to woodland paths and green fields, his imagination fired by glimpses of golden domes and glittering palaces in the distance on either hand, the Young Politician said:

"Let us, I beseech thee, turn aside from this comfortless road leading, thou knowest whither, but not I. Let us turn our backs upon duty and abandon ourselves to the delights and advantages which beckon from every grove and call to us from every shining hill. Let us, if so thou wilt, follow this beautiful path, which, as thou seest, hath a guide-board saying, 'Turn in here all ye who seek the Palace of Political Distinction.'"

"It is a beautiful path, my son," said the Old Politician, without either slackening his pace or turning his head, "and it leadeth among pleasant scenes. But the search for the Palace of Political Distinction is beset with one mighty peril."

"What is that?" said the Young Politician.

"The peril of finding it," the Old Politician replied, pushing on.

The Thoughtful Warden

The Warden of a Penitentiary was one day putting locks on the doors of all the cells when a mechanic said to him:

"Those locks can all be opened from the inside—you are very imprudent."

The Warden did not look up from his work, but said:

"If that is called imprudence, I wonder what would be called a thoughtful provision against the vicissitudes of fortune."

The Treasury and the Arms

A Public Treasury, feeling Two Arms lifting out its contents, exclaimed:

"Mr. Shareman, I move for a division."

"You seem to know something about parliamentary forms of speech," said the Two Arms.

"Yes," replied the Public Treasury, "I am familiar with the hauls of legislation."

The Christian Serpent

A Rattlesnake came home to his brood and said: "My children, gather about and receive your father's last blessing, and see how a Christian dies."

"What ails you, Father?" asked the Small Snakes.

"I have been bitten by the editor of a partisan journal," was the reply, accompanied by the ominous death-rattle.

The Broom of the Temple

The city of Gakwak being about to lose its character of capital of the province of Ukwuk, the Wampog issued a proclamation convening all the male residents in council in the Temple of Ul to devise means of defence. The first speaker thought the best policy would be to offer a fried jackass to the gods. The second suggested a public procession, headed by the Wampog himself, bearing the Holy Poker on a cushion of cloth-of-brass. Another thought that a scarlet mole should be buried alive in the public park and a suitable incantation chanted over the remains. The advice of the fourth was that the columns of the capitol be rubbed with oil of dog by a person having a moustache on the calf of his leg. When all the others had spoken an Aged Man rose and said:

"High and mighty Wampog and fellow-citizens, I have listened attentively to all the plans proposed. All seem wise, and I do not suffer myself to doubt that any one of them would be efficacious. Nevertheless, I cannot help thinking that if we would put an improved breed of polliwogs in our drinking water, construct shallower roadways, groom the street cows, offer the stranger within our gates a free choice between the poniard and the potion, and relinquish our private system of morals, the other measures of public safety would be needless."

The Aged Man was about to speak further, but the meeting informally adjourned in order to sweep the floor of the temple—for the men of Gakwak are the tidiest housewives in all that province. The last speaker was the broom.

The Critics

While bathing, Antinous was seen by Minerva, who was so enamoured of his beauty that, all armed as she happened to be, she descended from Olympus to woo him; but, unluckily displaying her shield, with the head of Medusa on it, she had the unhappiness to see the beautiful mortal turn to stone from catching a glimpse of it. She straightway ascended to ask Jove to restore him; but before this could be done a Sculptor and a Critic passed that way and espied him.

"This is a very bad Apollo," said the Sculptor: "the chest is too narrow, and one arm is at least a half-inch shorter than the other. The attitude is unnatural, and I may say impossible. Ah! my friend, you should see my statue of Antinous."

"In my judgment, the figure," said the Critic, "is

tolerably good, though rather Etrurian, but the expression of the face is decidedly Tuscan, and therefore false to nature. By the way, have you read my work on 'The Fallaciousness of the Aspectual in Art'?"

The Foolish Woman

A Married Woman, whose lover was about to reform by running away, procured a pistol and shot him dead.

"Why did you do that, Madam?" inquired a Policeman, sauntering by.

"Because," replied the Married Woman, "he was a wicked man, and had purchased a ticket to Chicago."

"My sister," said an adjacent Man of God, solemnly, "you cannot stop the wicked from going to Chicago by killing them."

Father and Son

"My boy," said an aged Father to his fiery and disobedient Son, "a hot temper is the soil of remorse. Promise me that when next you are angry you will count one hundred before you move or speak."

No sooner had the Son promised than he received a stinging blow from the paternal walking-stick, and by the time he had counted to seventy-five had the unhappiness to see the old man jump into a waiting cab and whirl away.

The Discontented Malefactor

A Judge having sentenced a Malefactor to the penitentiary was proceeding to point out to him the disadvantages of crime and the profit of reformation.

"Your Honour," said the Malefactor, interrupting,

"would you be kind enough to alter my punishment to ten years in the penitentiary and nothing else?"

"Why," said the Judge, surprised, "I have given you only three years!"

"Yes, I know," assented the Malefactor—"three years' imprisonment and the preaching. If you please, I should like to commute the preaching."

A Call to Quit

Seeing that his audiences were becoming smaller every Sunday, a Minister of the Gospel broke off in the midst of a sermon, descended the pulpit stairs, and walked on his hands down the central aisle of the church. He then remounted his feet, ascended to the pulpit, and resumed his discourse, making no allusion to the incident.

"Now," said he to himself, as he went home, "I shall have, henceforth, a large attendance and no snoring."

But on the following Friday he was waited upon by the Pillars of the Church, who informed him that in order to be in harmony with the New Theology and get full advantage of modern methods of Gospel interpretation they had deemed it advisable to make a change. They had therefore sent a call to Brother Jowjeetum-Fallal, the World-Renowned Hindoo Human Pin-Wheel, then holding forth in Hoopitup's circus. They were happy to say that the reverend gentleman had been moved by the Spirit to accept the call, and on the ensuing Sabbath would break the bread of life for the brethren or break his neck in the attempt.

The Man and the Lightning

A Man Running for Office was overtaken by Lightning.

"You see," said the Lightning, as it crept past him inch by inch, "I can travel considerably faster than you."

"Yes," the Man Running for Office replied, "but think how much longer I keep going!"

The Lassoed Bear

A Hunter who had lassoed a Bear was trying to disengage himself from the rope, but the slip-knot about his wrist would not yield, for the Bear was all the time pulling in the slack with his paws. In the midst of his trouble the Hunter saw a Showman passing by, and managed to attract his attention.

"What will you give me," he said, "for my Bear?"

"It will be some five or ten minutes," said the Showman, "before I shall want a fresh Bear, and it looks to me as if prices would fall during that time. I think I'll wait and watch the market."

"The price of this animal," the Hunter replied, "is down to bed-rock; you can have him for nothing a pound, spot cash, and I'll throw in the next one that I lasso. But the purchaser must remove the goods from the premises forthwith, to make room for three man-eating tigers, a cat-headed gorilla, and an armful of rattlesnakes."

But the Showman passed on, in maiden meditation, fancy free, and being joined soon afterward by the Bear, who was absently picking his teeth, it was inferred that they were not unacquainted.

The Ineffective Rooter

A Drunken Man was lying in the road with a bleeding nose, upon which he had fallen, when a Pig passed that way.

"You wallow fairly well," said the Pig, "but, my fine fellow, you have much to learn about rooting."

A Protagonist of Silver

Some Financiers who were whetting their tongues on their teeth because the Government had "struck down" silver, and were about to "inaugurate" a season of sweatshed, were addressed as follows by a Member of their honourable and warlike body:

"Comrades of the thunder and companions of death, I cannot but regard it as singularly fortunate that we who by conviction and sympathy are designated by nature as the champions of that fairest of her products, the white metal, should also, by a happy chance, be engaged mostly in the business of mining it. Nothing could be more appropriate than that those who from unselfish motives and elevated sentiments are doing battle for the people's rights and interests, should themselves be the chief beneficiaries of success. Therefore, O children of the earthquake and the storm, let us stand shoulder to shoulder, heart to heart, and pocket to pocket!"

This speech so pleased the other Members of the convention that, actuated by a magnanimous impulse, they sprang to their feet and left the hall. It was the first time they had ever been known to leave anything having value.

The Holy Deacon

An Itinerant Preacher who had wrought hard in the moral vineyard for several hours whispered to a Holy Deacon of the local church:

"Brother, these people know you, and your active support will bear fruit abundantly. Please pass the plate for me, and you shall have one fourth."

The Holy Deacon did so, and putting the money into his pocket waited till the congregation was dismissed and said goodnight.

"But the money, brother, the money that you collected!"
said the Itinerant Preacher.

"Nothing is coming to you," was the reply; "the Adversary has hardened their hearts, and one fourth is all they gave."

A Hasty Settlement

"Your Honour," said an Attorney, rising, "what is the present status of this case—as far as it has gone?"

"I have given a judgment for the residuary legatee under the will," said the Court, "put the costs upon the contestants, decided all questions relating to fees and other charges; and, in short, the estate in litigation has been settled, with all controversies, disputes, misunderstandings, and differences of opinion thereunto appertaining."

"Ah, yes, I see," said the Attorney, thoughtfully, "we are making progress—we are getting on famously."

"Progress?" echoed the Judge—"progress? Why, sir, the matter is concluded!"

"Exactly, exactly; it had to be concluded in order to give relevancy to the motion that I am about to make. Your Honour, I move that the judgment of the Court be set aside and the case reopened."

"Upon what ground, sir?" the Judge asked in surprise.

"Upon the ground," said the Attorney, "that after paying all fees and expenses of litigation and all charges against the estate there will still be something left."

"There may have been an error," said His Honour, thoughtfully—"the Court may have underestimated the value of the estate. The motion is taken under advisement."

The Wooden Guns

An Artillery Regiment of a State Militia applied to the Governor for wooden guns to practise with.

"Those," they explained, "will be cheaper than real ones."

"It shall not be said that I sacrificed efficiency to economy," said the Governor. "You shall have real guns."

"Thank you, thank you," cried the warriors, effusively. "We will take good care of them, and in the event of war return them to the arsenal."

The Reform School Board

The members of the School Board in Doosnoswair being suspected of appointing female teachers for an improper consideration, the people elected a Board composed wholly of women. In a few years the scandal was at an end; there were no female teachers in the Depàrtment.

The Poet's Doom

An Object was walking along the King's highway wrapped in meditation and with little else on, when he suddenly found himself at the gates of a strange city. On applying for admittance, he was arrested as a necessitator of ordinances, and taken before the King.

"Who are you," said the King, "and what is your business in life?"

"Snouter the Sneak," replied the Object, with ready invention; "pick-pocket."

The King was about to command him to be released when the Prime Minister suggested that the prisoner's fingers be examined. They were found greatly flattened and calloused at the ends.

"Ha!" cried the King; "I told you so!—he is addicted to counting syllables. This is a poet. Turn him over to the Lord High Dissuader from the Head Habit."

"My liege," said the Inventor-in-Ordinary of Ingenious Penalties, "I venture to suggest a keener affliction."

"Name it," the King said.

"Let him retain that head!"

It was so ordered.

The Noser and the Note

The Head Rifler of an insolvent bank, learning that it was about to be visited by the official Noser into Things, placed his own personal note for a large amount among its resources, and, gaily touching his guitar, awaited the inspection. When the Noser came to the note he asked, "What's this?"

"That," said the Assistant Pocketer of Deposits, "is one of our liabilities."

"A liability?" exclaimed the Noser. "Nay, nay, an asset. That is what you mean, doubtless."

"Therein you err," the Pocketer explained; "that note was written in the bank with our own pen, ink, and paper, and we have not paid a stationery bill for six months."

"Ah, I see," the Noser said, thoughtfully; "it is a liability. May I ask how you expect to meet it?"

"With fortitude, please God," answered the Assistant Pocketer, his eyes to Heaven raising—"with fortitude and a firm reliance on the laxity of the law."

"Enough, enough," exclaimed the faithful servant of the State, choking with emotion; "here is a certificate of solvency."

"And here is a bottle of ink," the grateful financier said, slipping it into the other's pocket; "it is all that we have."

The Cat and the King

A Cat was looking at a King, as permitted by the proverb.

"Well," said the monarch, observing her inspection of the royal person, "how do you like me?"

"I can imagine a King," said the Cat, "whom I should like better."

"For example?"

"The King of the Mice."

The sovereign was so pleased with the wit of the reply that he gave her permission to scratch his Prime Minister's eyes out.

The Literary Astronomer

The Director of an Observatory, who, with a thirty-six-inch refractor, had discovered the moon, hastened to an Editor, with a four-column account of the event.

"How much?" said the Editor, sententiously, without looking up from his essay on the circularity of the political horizon.

"One hundred and sixty dollars," replied the man who had discovered the moon.

"Not half enough," was the Editor's comment.

"Generous man!" cried the Astronomer, glowing with warm and elevated sentiments, "pay me, then, what you will."

"Great and good friend," said the Editor, blandly, looking up from his work, "we are far asunder, it seems. The paying is to be done by you."

The Director of the Observatory gathered up the manuscript and went away, explaining that it needed correction; he had neglected to dot an m.

The Lion and the Rattlesnake

A Man having found a Lion in his path undertook to subdue him by the power of the human eye; and near by was a Rattlesnake engaged in fascinating a small bird.

"How are you getting on, brother?" the Man called out to the other reptile, without removing his eyes from those of the Lion.

"Admirably," replied the serpent. "My success is assured; my victim draws nearer and nearer in spite of her efforts."

"And mine," said the Man, "draws nearer and nearer in spite of mine. Are you sure it is all right?"

"If you don't think so," the reptile replied as well as he then could, with his mouth full of bird, "you'd better give it up."

A half-hour later, the Lion, thoughtfully picking his teeth with his claws, told the Rattlesnake that he had never in all his varied experience in being subdued, seen a subduer try so earnestly to give it up. "But," he added, with a wide, significant smile, "I looked him into countenance."

The Man with No Enemies

An Inoffensive Person walking in a public place was assaulted by a Stranger with a Club, and severely beaten.

When the Stranger with a Club was brought to trial, the complainant said to the Judge:

"I do not know why I was assaulted; I have not an enemy in the world."

"That," said the defendant, "is why I struck him."

"Let the prisoner be discharged," said the Judge; "a man who has no enemies has no friends. The courts are not for such."

The Alderman and the Raccoon

"I see quite a number of rings on your tail," said an Alderman to a Raccoon that he met in a zoölogical garden.

"Yes," replied the Raccoon, "and I hear quite a number of tales on your ring."

The Alderman, being of a sensitive, retiring disposition, shrank from further comparison, and, strolling to another part of the garden, stole the camel.

The Flying-Machine

An Ingenious Man who had built a flying-machine invited a great concourse of people to see it go up. At the appointed moment, everything being ready, he boarded the car and turned on the power. The machine immediately broke through the massive substructure upon which it was builded, and sank out of sight into the earth, the aeronaut springing out barely in time to save himself.

"Well," said he, "I have done enough to demonstrate the correctness of my details. The defects," he added, with a look at the ruined brick-work, "are merely basic and fundamental."

Upon this assurance the people came forward with subscriptions to build a second machine.

The Angel's Tear

An Unworthy Man who had laughed at the woes of a Woman whom he loved, was bewailing his indiscretion in sackcloth-of-gold and ashes-of-roses, when the Angel of Compassion looked down upon him, saying:

"Poor mortal!—how unblest not to know the wickedness of laughing at another's misfortune!"

So saying, he let fall a great tear, which, encountering in its descent a current of cold air, was congealed into a hailstone. This struck the Unworthy Man on the head and set him rubbing that bruised organ vigorously with one hand while vainly attempting to expand an umbrella with the other.

Thereat the Angel of Compassion did most shamelessly and wickedly laugh.

The City of Political Distinction

Jamrach the Rich, being anxious to reach the City of Political Distinction before nightfall, arrived at a fork of the road and was undecided which branch to follow; so he consulted a Wise-Looking Person who sat by the wayside.

"Take *that* road," said the Wise-Looking Person, pointing it out; "it is known as the Political Highway."

"Thank you," said Jamrach, and was about to proceed.

"About how much do you thank me?" was the reply. "Do you suppose I am here for my health?"

As Jamrach had not become rich by stupidity, he handed something to his guide and hastened on, and soon came to a toll-gate kept by a Benevolent Gentleman, to whom he gave something, and was suffered to pass. A little farther along he came to a bridge across an imaginary stream, where a Civil Engineer (who had built the bridge) demanded something for interest on his investment, and it was forthcoming. It was growing late when Jamrach came to the margin of what appeared to be a lake of black ink, and there the road terminated. Seeing a Ferryman in his boat he paid something for his passage and was about to embark.

"No," said the Ferryman. "Put your neck in this noose, and I will tow you over. It is the only way," he added, seeing that the passenger was about to complain of the accommodations.

In due time he was dragged across, half strangled, and dreadfully beslubbered by the feculent waters. "There," said the Ferryman, hauling him ashore and disengaging him, "you are now in the City of Political Distinction. It has fifty millions of inhabitants, and as the colour of the Filthy Pool does not wash off, they all look exactly alike."

"Alas!" exclaimed Jamrach, weeping and bewailing the loss of all his possessions, paid out in tips and tolls; "I will go back with you."

"I don't think you will," said the Ferryman, pushing off; "this city is situated on the Island of the Unreturning."

The Party Over There

A Man in a Hurry, whose watch was at his lawyer's, asked a Grave Person the time of day.

"I heard you ask that Party Over There the same question," said the Grave Person. "What answer did he give you?"

"He said it was about three o'clock," replied the Man in a Hurry; "but he did not look at his watch, and as the sun is nearly down, I think it is later."

"The fact that the sun is nearly down," the Grave Person said, "is immaterial, but the fact that he did not consult his timepiece and make answer after due deliberation and consideration is fatal. The answer given," continued the Grave Person, consulting his own timepiece, "is of no effect, invalid, and absurd."

"What, then," said the Man in a Hurry, eagerly, "is the time of day?"

"The question is remanded to the Party Over There for a new answer," replied the Grave Person, returning his watch to his pocket and moving away with great dignity.

He was a Judge of an Appellate Court.

The Poetess of Reform

One pleasant day in the latter part of eternity, as the Shades of all the great writers were reposing upon beds of asphodel and moly in the Elysian fields, each happy in hearing from the lips of the others nothing but copious quotation from his own works (for so Jove had kindly bedeviled their ears), there came in among them with triumphant mien a Shade whom none knew. She (for the newcomer showed such evidences of sex as cropped hair and a manly stride) took a seat in their midst, and smiling a superior smile explained:

"After centuries of oppression I have wrested my rights from the grasp of the jealous gods. On earth I was the Poetess of Reform, and sang to inattentive ears. Now for an eternity of honour and glory."

But it was not to be so, and soon she was the unhappiest of mortals, vainly desirous to wander again in gloom by the infernal lakes. For Jove had not bedeviled her ears, and she heard from the lips of each blessed Shade an incessant flow of quotation from his own works. Moreover, she was denied the happiness of repeating her poems. She could not recall a line of them, for Jove had decreed that the memory of them abide in Pluto's painful domain, as a part of the apparatus.

The Unchanged Diplomatist

The republic of Madagonia had been long and well represented at the court of the King of Patagascar by an officer called a Dazie, but one day the Madagonian Parliament conferred upon him the superior rank of Dandee. The next day after being apprised of his new dignity he hastened to inform the King of Patagascar.

"Ah, yes, I understand," said the King; "you have been promoted and given increased pay and allowances. There was an appropriation?"

"Yes, your Majesty."

"And you have now two heads, have you not?"

"Oh, no, your Majesty—only one, I assure you."

"Indeed? And how many legs and arms?"

"Two of each, Sire—only two of each."

"And only one body?"

"Just a single body, as you perceive."

Thoughtfully removing his crown and scratching the royal head, the monarch was silent a moment, and then he said:

"I fancy that appropriation has been misapplicd. You seem to be about the same kind of idiot that you were before."

An Invitation

A Pious Person who had overcharged his paunch with dead bird by way of attesting his gratitude for escaping the many calamities which Heaven had sent upon others, fell asleep at table and dreamed. He thought he lived in a country where turkeys were the ruling class, and every year they held a feast to manifest their sense of Heaven's goodness in sparing their lives to kill them later. One day, about a week before one of these feasts, he met the Supreme Gobbler, who said:

"You will please get yourself into good condition for the Thanksgiving dinner."

"Yes, your Excellency," replied the Pious Person, delighted, "I shall come hungry, I assure you. It is no small privilege to dine with your Excellency."

The Supreme Gobbler eyed him for a moment in silence; then he said:

"As one of the lower domestic animals, you cannot be expected to know much, but you might know something. Since you do not, you will permit me to point out that being asked to dinner is one thing; being asked to dine is another and a different thing."

With this significant remark the Supreme Gobbler left him, and thenceforward the Pious Person dreamed of himself as white meat and dark until rudely awakened by decapitation.

The Ashes of Madame Blavatsky

The two brightest lights of Theosophy being in the same place at once in company with the Ashes of Madame Blavatsky, an Inquiring Soul thought the time propitious to learn something worth while. So he sat at the feet of one awhile, and then he sat awhile at the feet of the other, and at last he applied his ear to the keyhole of the casket containing the Ashes of Madame Blavatsky. When the Inquiring Soul had completed his course of instruction he declared himself the Ahkoond of Swat, fell into the baleful habit of standing on his head, and swore that the mother who bore him was a pragmatic paralogism. Wherefore he was held in high reverence, and when the two other gentlemen were hanged for lying the Theosophists elected him to the leadership of their Disastral Body, and after a quiet life and an honourable death by the kick of a jackass he was reincarnated as a Yellow Dog. As such he ate the Ashes of Madame Blavatsky, and Theosophy was no more.

The Opossum of the Future

One day an Opossum who had gone to sleep hanging from the highest branch of a tree by the tail, awoke and saw a large Snake wound about the limb, between him and the trunk of the tree.

"If I hold on," he said to himself, "I shall be swallowed; if I let go I shall break my neck."

But suddenly he bethought himself to dissemble.

"My perfected friend," he said, "my parental instinct recognises in you a noble evidence and illustration of the theory of development. You are the Opossum of the Future, the ultimate Fittest Survivor of our species, the ripe result of progressive prehensility—all tail!"

But the Snake, proud of his ancient eminence in Scriptural history, was strictly orthodox, and did not accept the scientific view.

The Life-Savers

Seventy-five Men presented themselves before the President of the Humane Society and demanded the great gold medal for life-saving.

"Why, yes," said the President; "by diligent effort so many men must have saved a considerable number of lives. How many did you save?"

"Seventy-five, sir," replied their Spokesman.

"Ah, yes, that is one each—very good work—very good work, indeed," the President said. "You shall not only have the Society's great gold medal, but its recommendation for employment at the various life-boat stations along the coast. But how did you save so many lives?"

The Spokesman of the Men replied:

"We are officers of the law, and have just returned from the pursuit of two murderous outlaws."

The Australian Grasshopper

A Distinguished Naturalist was travelling in Australia, when he saw a Kangaroo in session and flung a stone at it. The Kangaroo immediately adjourned, tracing against the sunset sky a parabolic curve spanning seven provinces, and evanished below the horizon. The Distinguished Naturalist looked interested, but said nothing for an hour; then he said to his native Guide:

"You have pretty wide meadows here, I suppose?"

"No, not very wide," the Guide answered; "about the same as in England and America."

After another long silence the Distinguished Naturalist said:

"The hay which we shall purchase for our horses this evening—I shall expect to find the stalks about fifty feet long. Am I right?"

"Why, no," said the Guide; "a foot or two is about the usual length of our hay. What can you be thinking of?"

The Distinguished Naturalist made no immediate reply, but later, as in the shades of night they journeyed through the desolate vastness of the Great Lone Land, he broke the silence:

"I was thinking," he said, "of the uncommon magnitude of that grasshopper."

The Pavior

An Author saw a Labourer hammering stones into the pavement of a street, and approaching him said:

"My friend, you seem weary. Ambition is a hard task-master."

"I'm working for Mr. Jones, sir," the Labourer replied.

"Well, cheer up," the Author resumed; "fame comes at the most unexpected times. To-day you are poor, obscure, and disheartened, and to-morrow the world may be ringing with your name."

"What are you giving me?" the Labourer said. "Cannot an honest pavior perform his work in peace, and get his money for it, and his living by it, without others talking rot about ambition and hopes of fame?"

"Cannot an honest writer?" said the Author.

The Tried Assassin

An Assassin being put upon trial in a New England court, his Counsel rose and said: "Your Honour, I move for a discharge on the ground of 'once in jeopardy': my client has been already tried for that murder and acquitted."

"In what court?" asked the Judge.

"In the Superior Court of San Francisco," the Counsel replied.

"Let the trial proceed—your motion is denied," said the Judge. "An Assassin is not in jeopardy when tried in California."

The Bumbo of Jiam

The Pahdour of Patagascar and the Gookul of Madagonia were disputing about an island which both claimed. Finally, at the suggestion of the International League of Cannon Founders, which had important branches in both countries, they decided to refer their claims to the Bumbo of Jiam, and abide by his judgment. In settling the preliminaries of the arbitration they had, however, the misfortune to disagree, and appealed to arms. At the end of a long and disastrous war, when both sides were exhausted and bankrupt, the Bumbo of Jiam intervened in the interest of peace.

"My great and good friends," he said to his brother sovereigns, "it will be advantageous to you to learn that some questions are more complex and perilous than others, presenting a greater number of points upon which it is possible to differ. For four generations your royal predecessors disputed about possession of that island, without falling out. Beware, oh, beware the perils of international arbitration!—against which I feel it my duty to protect you henceforth."

So saying, he annexed both countries, and after a long, peaceful, and happy reign was poisoned by his Prime Minister.

The Two Poets

Two Poets were quarrelling for the Apple of Discord and the Bone of Contention, for they were very hungry.

"My sons," said Apollo, "I will part the prizes between you. You," he said to the First Poet, "excel in Art—take the Apple. And you," he said to the Second Poet, "in Imagination—take the Bone."

"To Art the best prize!" said the First Poet, triumphantly, and endeavouring to devour his award broke all his teeth. The Apple was a work of Art.

"That shows our Master's contempt for mere Art," said the Second Poet, grinning.

Thereupon he attempted to gnaw his Bone, but his teeth passed through it without resistance. It was an imaginary Bone.

The Thistles upon the Grave

A Mind Reader made a wager that he would be buried alive and remain so for six months, then be dug up alive. In order to secure the grave against secret disturbance, it was sown with thistles. At the end of three months, the Mind Reader lost his money. He had come up to eat the thistles.

The Shadow of the Leader

A Political Leader was walking out one sunny day, when he observed his Shadow leaving him and walking rapidly away.

"Come back here, you scoundrel," he cried.

"If I had been a scoundrel," answered the Shadow, increasing its speed, "I should not have left you."

The Sagacious Rat

A Rat that was about to emerge from his hole caught a glimpse of a Cat waiting for him, and descending to the colony at the bottom of the hole invited a Friend to join him in a visit to a neighbouring corn-bin. "I would have gone alone," he said, "but could not deny myself the pleasure of such distinguished company."

"Very well," said the Friend, "I will go with you. Lead on."

"Lead?" exclaimed the other. "What! *I* precede so great and illustrious a rat as you? No, indeed—after you, sir, after you."

Pleased with this great show of deference, the Friend went ahead, and, leaving the hole first, was caught by the Cat, who immediately trotted away with him. The other then went out unmolested.

The Member and the Soap

A member of the Kansas Legislature meeting a Cake of Soap was passing it by without recognition, but the Cake of Soap insisted on stopping and shaking hands. Thinking it might possibly be in the enjoyment of the elective franchise, he gave it a cordial and earnest grasp. On letting it go he observed that a portion of it adhered to his fingers, and running to a brook in great alarm he proceeded to wash it off. In doing so he necessarily got some on the other hand, and when he had finished washing, both were so white that he went to bed and sent for a physician.

Alarm and Pride

"Good-morning, my friend," said Alarm to Pride; "how are you this morning?"

"Very tired," replied Pride, seating himself on a stone by the wayside and mopping his steaming brow. "The politicians are wearing me out by pointing to their dirty records with *me*, when they could as well use a stick."

Alarm sighed sympathetically, and said:

"It is pretty much the same way here. Instead of using an opera-glass they view the acts of their opponents with *me*!"

As these patient drudges were mingling their tears, they were notified that they must go on duty again, for one of the political parties had nominated a thief and was about to hold a gratification meeting.

A Causeway

A Rich Woman having returned from abroad disembarked at the foot of Knee-deep Street, and was about to walk to her hotel through the mud.

"Madam," said a Policeman, "I cannot permit you to do that; you would soil your shoes and stockings."

"Oh, that is of no importance, really," replied the Rich Woman, with a cheerful smile.

"But, madam, it is needless; from the wharf to the hotel, as you observe, extends an unbroken line of prostrate newspaper men who crave the honour of having you walk upon them."

"In that case," she said, seating herself in a doorway and unlocking her satchel, "I shall have to put on my rubber boots."

Two in Trouble

Meeting a fat and patriotic Statesman on his way to Washington to beseech the President for an office, an idle Tramp accosted him and begged twenty-five cents with which to buy a suit of clothes.

"Melancholy wreck," said the Statesman, "what brought you to this state of degradation? Liquor, I suppose."

"I am temperate to the verge of absurdity," replied the Tramp. "My foible was patriotism; I was ruined by the baneful habit of trying to serve my country. What ruined you?"

"Indolence."

The Witch's Steed

A Broomstick which had long served a witch as a steed complained of the nature of its employment, which it thought degrading.

"Very well," said the Witch, "I will give you work in which you will be associated with intellect—you will come in contact with brains. I shall present you to a housewife."

"What!" said the Broomstick, "do you consider the hands of a housewife intellectual?"

"I referred," said the Witch, "to the head of her good man."

The All Dog

A Lion seeing a Poodle fell into laughter at the ridiculous spectacle.

"Who ever saw so small a beast?" he said.

"It is very true," said the Poodle, with austere dignity, "that I am small; but, sir, I beg to observe that I am all dog."

The Farmer's Friend

A Great Philanthropist who had thought of himself in connection with the Presidency and had introduced a bill into Congress requiring the Government to loan every voter all the money that he needed, on his personal security, was explaining to a Sunday-school at a railway station how much he had done for the country, when an angel looked down from Heaven and wept.

"For example," said the Great Philanthropist, watching the teardrops pattering in the dust, "these early rains are of incalculable advantage to the farmer."

Physicians Two

A Wicked Old Man finding himself ill sent for a Physician, who prescribed for him and went away. Then the Wicked Old Man sent for another Physician, saying nothing of the first, and an entirely different treatment was ordered. This continued for some weeks, the physicians visiting him on alternate days and treating him for two different disorders, with constantly enlarging doses of medicine and more and more rigorous nursing. But one day they accidently met at his bedside while he slept, and the truth coming out a violent quarrel ensued.

"My good friends," said the patient, awakened by the noise of the dispute, and apprehending the cause of it, "pray be more reasonable. If I could for weeks endure you both, can you not for a little while endure each other? I have been well for ten days, but have remained in bed in the hope of gaining by repose the strength that would justify me in taking your medicines. So far I have touched none of it."

The Overlooked Factor

A Man that owned a fine Dog, and by a careful selection of its mate had bred a number of animals but a little lower than the angels, fell in love with his washer-woman, married her, and reared a family of dolts.

"Alas!" he exclaimed, contemplating the melancholy result, "had I but chosen a mate for myself with half the care that I did for my Dog I should now be a proud and happy father."

"I'm not so sure of that," said the Dog, overhearing the lament. "There's a difference, certainly, between your whelps and mine, but I venture to flatter myself that it is not due altogether to the mothers. You and I are not entirely alike ourselves."

A Racial Parallel

Some White Christians engaged in driving Chinese Heathens out of an American town found a newspaper published in Peking in the Chinese tongue, and compelled one of their victims to translate an editorial. It turned out to be an appeal to the people of the Province of Pang Ki to drive the foreign devils out of the country and burn their dwellings and churches. At this evidence of Mongolian barbarity the White Christians were so greatly incensed that they carried out their original design.

The Honest Cadi

A Robber who had plundered a Merchant of one thousand pieces of gold was taken before the Cadi, who asked him if he had anything to say why he should not be decapitated.

"Your Honour," said the Robber, "I could do no otherwise than take the money, for Allah made me that way."

"Your defence is ingenious and sound," said the Cadi, "and I must acquit you of criminality. Unfortunately, Allah has made me so that I must also take off your head—unless," he added, thoughtfully, "you offer me half of the gold; for He made me weak under temptation."

Thereupon the Robber put five hundred pieces of gold into the Cadi's hand.

"Good," said the Cadi. "I shall now remove but one half your head. To show my trust in your discretion I shall leave intact the half you talk with."

The Kangaroo and the Zebra

A Kangaroo hopping awkwardly along with some bulky object concealed in her pouch met a Zebra, and desirous of keeping his attention upon himself, said:

"Your costume looks as if you might have come out of the penitentiary."

"Appearances are deceitful," replied the Zebra, smiling in the consciousness of a more insupportable wit, "or I should have to think that you had come out of the Legislature."

A Matter of Method

A Philosopher seeing a Fool beating his Donkey, said:

"Abstain, my son, abstain, I implore. Those who resort to violence shall suffer from violence."

"That," said the Fool, diligently belabouring the animal, "is what I'm trying to teach this beast—which has kicked me."

"Doubtless," said the Philosopher to himself, as he walked away, "the wisdom of fools is no deeper nor truer than ours, but they really do seem to have a more impressive way of imparting it."

The Man of Principle

During a shower of rain the Keeper of a Zoölogical garden observed a Man of Principle crouching beneath the belly of the ostrich, which had drawn itself up to its full height to sleep.

"Why, my dear sir," said the Keeper, "if you fear to get wet, you'd better creep into the pouch of yonder female kangaroo—the *Saltarix mackintosha*—for if that ostrich wakes he will kick you to death in a minute."

"I can't help that," the Man of Principle replied, with that lofty scorn of practical considerations distinguishing his species. "He may kick me to death if he wish, but until he does he shall give me shelter from the storm. He has swallowed my umbrella."

The Returned Californian

A Man was hanged by the neck until he was dead.

"Whence do you come?" Saint Peter asked when the Man presented himself at the gate of Heaven.

"From California," replied the applicant.

"Enter, my son, enter; you bring joyous tidings."

When the Man had vanished inside, Saint Peter took his memorandum-tablet and made the following entry:

February 16, 1893. California occupied by the Christians.

The Compassionate Physician

A Kind-hearted Physician sitting at the bedside of a patient afflicted with an incurable and painful disease, heard a noise behind him, and turning saw a cat laughing at the feeble efforts of a wounded mouse to drag itself out of the room.

"You cruel beast!" cried he. "Why don't you kill it at once, like a lady?"

Rising, he kicked the cat out of the door, and picking up the mouse compassionately put it out of its misery by pulling off its head. Recalled to the bedside by the moans of his patient, the Kind-hearted Physician administered a stimulant, a tonic, and a nutrient, and went away.

Two of the Damned

Two Blighted Beings, haggard, lachrymose, and detested, met on a blasted heath in the light of a struggling moon.

"I wish you a merry Christmas," said the First Blighted Being, in a voice like that of a singing tomb.

"And I you a happy New Year," responded the Second Blighted Being, with the accent of a penitent accordion.

They then fell upon each other's neck and wept scalding rills down each other's spine in token of their banishment to the Realm of Ineffable Bosh. For one of these accursed creatures was the First of January, and the other the Twenty-fifth of December.

The Austere Governor

A Governor visiting a State prison was implored by a Convict to pardon him.

"What are you in for?" asked the Governor.

"I held a high office," the Convict humbly replied, "and sold subordinate appointments."

"Then I decline to interfere," said the Governor, with asperity: "a man who abuses his office by making it serve a private end and purvey a personal advantage is unfit to be free. By the way, Mr. Warden," he added to that official, as the Convict slunk away, "in appointing you to this position, I was given to understand that your friends could make the Shikane county delegation to the next State convention solid for—for the present Administration. Was I rightly informed?"

"You were, sir."

"Very well, then, I will bid you good-day. Please be so good as to appoint my nephew Night Chaplain and Reminder of Mothers and Sisters."

Religions of Error

Hearing a sound of strife, a Christian in the Orient asked his Dragoman the cause of it.

"The Buddhists are cutting Mohammedan throats," the Dragoman replied, with oriental composure.

"I did not know," remarked the Christian, with scientific interest, "that that would make so much noise."

"The Mohammedans are cutting Buddhist throats, too," added the Dragoman.

"It is astonishing," mused the Christian, "how violent and how general are religious animosities. Everywhere in the world the devotees of each local faith abhor the devotees of every other, and abstain from murder only so long as they dare not commit it. And the strangest thing about it is that all religions are erroneous and mischievous excepting mine. Mine, thank God, is true and benign."

So saying he visibly smugged and went off to telegraph for a brigade of cutthroats to protect Christian interests.

The Penitent Elector

A Person belonging to the Society for Passing Resolutions of Respect for the Memory of Deceased Members having died received the customary attention.

"Good Heavens!" exclaimed a Sovereign Elector, on hearing the resolutions read, "what a loss to the nation! And to think that I once voted against that angel for Inspector of Gate-latches in Public Squares!"

In remorse the Sovereign Elector deprived himself of political influence by learning to read.

The Tail of the Sphinx

A Dog of a taciturn disposition said to his Tail:
"Whenever I am angry, you rise and bristle; when I am pleased, you wag; when I am alarmed, you tuck yourself in out of danger. You are too mercurial—you disclose all my emotions. My notion is that tails are given to conceal thought. It is my dearest ambition to be as impassive as the Sphinx."

"My friend, you must recognise the laws and limitations of your being," replied the Tail, with flexions appropriate to the sentiments uttered, "and try to be great some other way. The Sphinx has one hundred and fifty qualifications for impassiveness which you lack."

"What are they?" the Dog asked.

"One hundred and forty-nine tons of sand on her tail."

"And——?"

"A stone tail."

A Prophet of Evil

An Undertaker Who Was a Member of a Trust saw a Man Leaning on a Spade, and asked him why he was not at work.

"Because," said the Man Leaning on a Spade, "I belong to the Gravediggers' National Extortion Society, and we have decided to limit the production of graves and get more money for the reduced output. We have a corner in graves and propose to work it to the best advantage."

"My friend," said the Undertaker Who Was a Member of a Trust, "this is a most hateful and injurious scheme. If people cannot be assured of graves, I fear they will no longer die, and the best interests of civilisation will wither like a frosted leaf."

And blowing his eyes upon his handkerchief, he walked away lamenting.

The Crew of the Life-boat

The Gallant Crew at a life-saving station were about to launch their life-boat for a spin along the coast when they discovered, but a little distance away, a capsized vessel with a dozen men clinging to her keel.

"We are fortunate," said the Gallant Crew, "to have seen that in time. Our fate might have been the same as theirs."

So they hauled the life-boat back into its house, and were spared to the service of their country.

A Treaty of Peace

Through massacres of each other's citizens China and the United States had been four times plunged into devastating wars, when, in the year 1994, arose a Philosopher in Madagascar, who laid before the Governments of the two distracted countries the following *modus vivendi* :

> Massacres are to be sternly forbidden as heretofore; but any citizen or subject of either country disobeying the injunction is to detach the scalps of all persons massacred and deposit them with a local officer designated to receive and preserve them and sworn to keep and render a true account thereof. At the conclusion of each massacre in either country, or as soon thereafter as practicable, or at stated regular periods, as may be provided by treaty, there shall be an exchange of scalps between the two Governments, scalp for scalp, without regard to sex or age; the Government having the greatest number is to be taxed on the excess at the rate of $1000 a scalp, and the other Government credited with the amount. Once in every decade there shall be a general settlement, when the balance due shall be paid to the creditor nation in Mexican dollars.

The plan was adopted, the necessary treaty made, with legislation to carry out its provisions; the Madagascarene Philosopher took his seat in the Temple of Immortality, and

Peace spread her white wings over the two nations, to the unspeakable defiling of her plumage.

The Nightside of Character

A Gifted and Honourable Editor, who by practice of his profession had acquired wealth and distinction, applied to an Old Friend for the hand of his daughter in marriage.

"With all my heart, and God bless you!" said the Old Friend, grasping him by both hands. "It is a greater honour than I had dared to hope for."

"I knew what your answer would be," replied the Gifted and Honourable Editor. "And yet," he added, with a sly smile, "I feel that I ought to give you as much knowledge of my character as I possess. In this scrap-book is such testimony relating to my shady side, as I have within the past ten years been able to cut from the columns of my competitors in the business of elevating humanity to a higher plane of mind and morals—my 'loathsome contemporaries.'"

Laying the book on a table, he withdrew in high spirits to make arrangements for the wedding. Three days later he received the scrap-book from a messenger, with a note warning him never again to darken his Old Friend's door.

"See!" the Gifted and Honourable Editor exclaimed, pointing to that injunction—"I am a painter and grainer!"

And he was led away to the Asylum for the Indiscreet.

The Faithful Cashier

The Cashier of a bank having defaulted was asked by the Directors what he had done with the money taken.

"I am greatly surprised by such a question," said the Cashier; "it sounds as if you suspected me of selfishness. Gentlemen, I applied that money to the purpose for which I took it; I paid it as an initiation fee and one year's dues in advance to the Treasurer of the Cashiers' Mutual Defence Association."

"What is the object of that organisation?" the Directors inquired.

"When any one of its members is under suspicion," replied the Cashier, "the Association undertakes to clear his character by submitting evidence that he was never a prominent member of any church, nor foremost in Sunday-school work."

Recognising the value to the bank of a spotless reputation for its officers, the President drew his check for the amount of the shortage and the Cashier was restored to favour.

The Circular Clew

A Detective searching for the murderer of a dead man was accosted by a Clew.

"Follow me," said the Clew, "and there's no knowing what you may discover."

So the Detective followed the Clew a whole year through a thousand sinuosities, and at last found himself in the office of the Morgue.

"There!" said the Clew, pointing to the open register.

The Detective eagerly scanned the page, and found an official statement that the deceased was dead. Thereupon he hastened to Police Headquarters to report progress. The Clew, meanwhile, sauntered among the busy haunts of men, arm in arm with an Ingenious Theory.

The Devoted Widow

A Widow weeping on her husband's grave was approached by an Engaging Gentleman who, in a respectful manner, assured her that he had long entertained for her the most tender feelings.

"Wretch!" cried the Widow. "Leave me this instant! Is this a time to talk to me of love?"

"I assure you, madam, that I had not intended to disclose my affection," the Engaging Gentleman humbly explained, "but the power of your beauty has overcome my discretion."

"You should see me when I have not been crying," said the Widow.

The Hardy Patriots

A Dispenser-Elect of Patronage gave notice through the newspapers that applicants for places would be given none until he should assume the duties of his office.

"You are exposing yourself to a grave danger," said a Lawyer.

"How so?" the Dispenser-Elect inquired.

"It will be nearly two months," the Lawyer answered, "before the day that you mention. Few patriots can live so long without eating, and some of the applicants will be compelled to go to work in the meantime. If that kills them, you will be liable to prosecution for murder."

"You underrate their powers of endurance," the official replied.

"What!" said the Lawyer, "you think they can stand work?"

"No," said the other—"hunger."

The Humble Peasant

An Office Seeker whom the President had ordered out of Washington was watering the homeward highway with his tears.

"Ah," he said, "how disastrous is ambition! how unsatisfying its rewards! how terrible its disappointments! Behold yonder peasant tilling his field in peace and contentment! He rises with the lark, passes the day in wholesome toil, and lies down at night to pleasant dreams. In the mad struggle for place and power he has no part; the roar of the strife reaches his ear like the distant murmur of the ocean. Happy, thrice happy man! I will approach him and bask in the sunshine of his humble felicity. Peasant, all hail!"

Leaning upon his rake, the Peasant returned the salutation with a nod, but said nothing.

"My friend," said the Office Seeker, "you see before you the wreck of an ambitious man—ruined by the pursuit of place and power. This morning when I set out from the national capital——"

"Stranger," the Peasant interrupted, "if you're going back there soon maybe you wouldn't mind using your influence to make me Postmaster at Smith's Corners."

The traveller passed on.

The Various Delegation

The King of Wideout having been offered the sovereignty of Wayoff, sent for the Three Persons who had made the offer, and said to them:

"I am extremely obliged to you, but before accepting so great a responsibility I must ascertain the sentiments of the people of Wayoff."

"Sire," said the Spokesman of the Three Persons, "they stand before you."

"Indeed!" said the King; "are you, then, the people of Wayoff?"

"Yes, your Majesty."

"There are not many of you," the King said, attentively regarding them with the royal eye, "and you are not so very large; I hardly think you are a quorum. Moreover, I never heard of you until you came here; whereas Wayoff is noted for the quality of its pork and contains hogs of distinction. I shall send a Commissioner to ascertain the sentiments of the hogs."

The Three Persons, bowing profoundly, backed out of the presence; but soon afterwards they desired another audience, and, on being readmitted, said, through their Spokesman:

"May it please your Majesty, we are the hogs."

The No Case

A Statesman who had been indicted by an unfeeling Grand Jury was arrested by a Sheriff and thrown into jail. As this was abhorrent to his fine spiritual nature, he sent for the District Attorney and asked that the case against him be dismissed.

"Upon what grounds?" asked the District Attorney.

"Lack of evidence to convict," replied the accused.

"Do you happen to have the lack with you?" the official asked. "I should like to see it."

"With pleasure," said the other; "here it is."

So saying he handed the other a check, which the District Attorney carefully examined, and then pronounced it the most complete absence of both proof and presumption that he had ever seen. He said it would acquit the oldest man in the world.

A Harmless Visitor

At a meeting of the Golden League of Mystery a Woman was discovered, writing in a note-book. A member directed the attention of the Superb High Chairman to her, and she was asked to explain her presence there, and what she was doing.

"I came in for my own pleasure and instruction," she said, "and was so struck by the wisdom of the speakers that I could not help making a few notes."

"Madam," said the Superb High Chairman, "we have no objection to visitors if they will pledge themselves not to publish anything they hear. Are you—on your honour as a lady, now, madam—are you not connected with some news-paper?"

"Good gracious, no!" cried the Woman, earnestly. "Why, sir, I am an officer of the Women's Press Association!"

She was permitted to remain, and presented with resolutions of apology.

The Judge and the Rash Act

A Judge who had for years looked in vain for an oppor-tunity for infamous distinction, but whom no litigant thought worth bribing, sat one day upon the Bench, lamenting his hard lot, and threatening to put an end to his life if business did not improve. Suddenly he found himself confronted by a dreadful figure clad in a shroud, whose pallor and stony eyes smote him with a horrible apprehension.

"Who are you," he faltered, "and why do you come here?"

"I am the Rash Act," was the sepulchral reply; "you may commit me."

"No," the Judge said, thoughtfully, "no, that would be quite irregular. I do not sit to-day as a committing magis-trate."

The Prerogative of Might

A Slander travelling rapidly through the land upon its joyous mission was accosted by a Retraction and commanded to halt and be killed.

"Your career of mischief is at an end," said the Retraction, drawing his club, rolling up his sleeves, and spitting on his hands.

"Why should you slay me?" protested the Slander. "Whatever my intentions were, I have been innocuous, for you have dogged my strides and counteracted my influence."

"Dogged your grandmother!" said the Retraction, with contemptuous vulgarity of speech. "In the order of nature it is appointed that we two shall never travel the same road."

"How then," the Slander asked, triumphantly, "have you overtaken me?"

"I have not," replied the Retraction; "we have accidentally met. I came round the world the other way."

But when he tried to execute his fell purpose he found that in the order of nature it was appointed that he himself perish miserably in the encounter.

An Inflated Ambition

The President of a great Corporation went into a dry-goods shop and saw a placard which read:

"If You Don't See What You Want, Ask For It."

Approaching the shopkeeper, who had been narrowly observing him as he read the placard, he was about to speak, when the shopkeeper called to a salesman:

"John, show this gentleman the world."

Rejected Services

A Heavy Operator overtaken by a Reverse of Fortune was bewailing his sudden fall from affluence to indigence.

"Do not weep," said the Reverse of Fortune. "You need not suffer alone. Name any one of the men who have opposed your schemes, and I will overtake *him*."

"It is hardly worth while," said the victim, earnestly. "Not a soul of them has a cent!"

The Power of the Scalawag

A Forestry Commissioner had just felled a giant tree when, seeing an honest man approaching, he dropped his axe and fled. The next day when he cautiously returned to get his axe, he found the following lines pencilled on the stump:

> *What nature reared by centuries of toil,*
> *A scalawag in half a day can spoil;*
> *An equal fate for him may Heaven provide—*
> *Damned in the moment of his tallest pride.*

At Large—One Temper

A Turbulent Person was brought before a Judge to be tried for an assault with intent to commit murder, and it was proved that he had been variously obstreperous without apparent provocation, had affected the peripheries of several luckless fellow-citizens with the trunk of a small tree, and subsequently cleaned out the town. While trying to palliate these misdeeds, the defendant's Attorney turned suddenly to the Judge, saying:

"Did your Honour ever lose your temper?"

"I fine you twenty-five dollars for contempt of court!" roared the Judge, in wrath. "How dare you mention the loss of my temper in connection with this case?"

After a moment's silence the Attorney said, meekly:

"I thought my client might perhaps have found it."

The Seeker and the Sought

A Politician seeing a fat Turkey which he wanted for dinner, baited a hook with a grain of corn and dragged it before the fowl at the end of a long and almost invisible line. When the Turkey had swallowed the hook, the Politician ran, drawing the creature after him.

"Fellow-citizens," he cried, addressing some turkey-breeders whom he met, "you observe that the man does not seek the bird, but the bird seeks the man. For this unsolicited and unexpected dinner I thank you with all my heart."

His Fly-Speck Majesty

A Distinguished Advocate of Republican Institutions was seen pickling his shins in the ocean.

"Why don't you come out on dry land?" said the Spectator. "What are you in there for?"

"Sir," replied the Distinguished Advocate of Republican Institutions, "a ship is expected, bearing His Majesty the King of the Fly-Speck Islands, and I wish to be the first to grasp the crowned hand."

"But," said the Spectator, "you said in your famous speech before the Society for the Prevention of the Protrusion of Nail Heads from Plank Sidewalks that Kings were blood-smeared oppressors and hell-bound loafers."

"My dear sir," said the Distinguished Advocate of Republican Institutions, without removing his eyes from the horizon, "you wander away into the strangest irrelevancies! I spoke of Kings in the abstract."

The Pugilist's Diet

The Trainer of a Pugilist consulted a Physician regarding the champion's diet.

"Beef-steaks are too tender," said the Physician; "have his meat cut from the neck of a bull."

"I thought the steaks more digestible," the Trainer explained.

"That is very true," said the Physician; "but they do not sufficiently exercise the chin."

The Old Man and the Pupil

A Beautiful Old Man, meeting a Sunday-school Pupil, laid his hand tenderly upon the lad's head, saying: "Listen, my son, to the words of the wise and heed the advice of the righteous."

"All right," said the Sunday-school Pupil; "go ahead."

"Oh, I haven't anything to do with it myself," said the Beautiful Old Man. "I am only observing one of the customs of the age. I am a pirate."

And when he had taken his hand from the lad's head, the latter observed that his hair was full of clotted blood. Then the Beautiful Old Man went his way, instructing other youth.

The Deceased and His Heirs

A Man died leaving a large estate and many sorrowful relations who claimed it. After some years, when all but one had had judgment given against them, that one was awarded the estate, which he asked his Attorney to have appraised.

"There is nothing to appraise," said the Attorney, pocketing his last fee.

"Then," said the Successful Claimant, "what good has all this litigation done me?"

"You have been a good client to me," the Attorney replied, gathering up his books and papers, "but I must say you betray a surprising ignorance of the purpose of litigation."

The Politicians and the Plunder

Several Political Entities were dividing the spoils.

"I will take the management of the prisons," said a Decent Respect for Public Opinion, "and make a radical change."

"And I," said the Blotted Escutcheon, "will retain my present general connection with affairs, while my friend here, the Soiled Ermine, will remain in the Judiciary."

The Political Pot said it would not boil any more unless replenished from the Filthy Pool.

The Cohesive Power of Public Plunder quietly remarked that the two bosses would, he supposed, naturally be his share.

"No," said the Depth of Degradation, "they have already fallen to me."

The Man and the Wart

A Person with a Wart on His Nose met a Person Similarly Afflicted, and said:

"Let me propose your name for membership in the Imperial Order of Abnormal Proboscidians, of which I am the High Noble Toby and Surreptitious Treasurer. Two months ago I was the only member. One month ago there were two. To-day we number four Emperors of the Abnormal Proboscis in good standing—doubles every four weeks, see? That's geometrical progression—you know how that piles up. In a year and a half every man in California will have a wart on his Nose. Powerful Order! Initiation, five dollars."

"My friend," said the Person Similarly Afflicted, "here are five dollars. Keep my name off your books."

"Thank you kindly," the Man with a Wart on His Nose replied, pocketing the money; "it is just the same to us as if you joined. Good-by."

He went away, but in a little while he was back.

"I quite forgot to mention the monthly dues," he said.

The Divided Delegation

A Delegation at Washington went to a New President, and said:

"Your Excellency, we are unable to agree upon a Favourite Son to represent us in your Cabinet."

"Then," said the New President, "I shall have to lock you up until you do agree."

So the Delegation was cast into the deepest dungeon beneath the moat, where it maintained a divided mind for many weeks, but finally reconciled its differences and asked to be taken before the New President.

"My child," said he, "nothing is so beautiful as harmony. My Cabinet Selections were all made before our former interview, but you have supplied a noble instance of patriotism in subordinating your personal preferences to the general good. Go now to your beautiful homes and be happy."

It is not recorded that the Delegation was happy.

A Forfeited Right

The Chief of the Weather Bureau having predicted a fine day, a Thrifty Person hastened to lay in a large stock of umbrellas, which he exposed for sale on the sidewalk; but the weather remained clear, and nobody would buy. Thereupon the Thrifty Person brought an action against the Chief of the Weather Bureau for the cost of the umbrellas.

"Your Honour," said the defendant's attorney, when the case was called, "I move that this astonishing action be dismissed. Not only is my client in no way responsible for the loss, but he distinctly foreshadowed the very thing that caused it."

"That is just it, your Honour," replied the counsel for the plaintiff; "the defendant by making a correct forecast fooled my client in the only way that he could do so. He has lied so much and so notoriously that he has neither the legal nor moral right to tell the truth."

Judgment for the plaintiff.

Revenge

An Insurance Agent was trying to induce a Hard Man to Deal With to take out a policy on his house. After listening to him for an hour, while he painted in vivid colours the extreme danger of fire consuming the house, the Hard Man to Deal With said: "Do you really think it likely that my house will burn down inside the time that policy will run?"

"Certainly," replied the Insurance Agent; "have I not been trying all this time to convince you that I do?"

"Then," said the Hard Man to Deal With, "why are you so anxious to have your Company bet me money that it will not?"

The Agent was silent and thoughtful for a moment; then he drew the other apart into an unfrequented place and whispered in his ear: "My friend, I will impart to you a dark secret. Years ago the Company betrayed my sweetheart by promise of marriage. Under an assumed name I have wormed myself into its service for revenge; and as there is a heaven above us, I will have its heart's blood!"

An Optimist

Two Frogs in the belly of a snake were considering their altered circumstances.

"This is pretty hard luck," said one.

"Don't jump to conclusions," the other said; "we are out of the wet and provided with board and lodging."

"With lodging, certainly," said the First Frog; "but I don't see the board."

"You are a croaker," the other explained. "We are ourselves the board."

A Valuable Suggestion

A Big Nation having a quarrel with a Little Nation, resolved to terrify its antagonist by a grand naval demonstration in the latter's principal port. So the Big Nation assembled all its ships of war from all over the world, and was about to send them three hundred and fifty thousand miles to the place of rendezvous, when the President of the Big Nation received the following note from the President of the Little Nation:

> My great and good friend, I hear that you are going to show us your navy, in order to impress us with a sense of your power. How needless the expense! To prove to you that we already know all about it, I inclose herewith a list and description of all the ships you have.

The great and good friend was so struck by the hard sense of the letter that he kept his navy at home, and saved one thousand million dollars. This economy enabled him to buy a satisfactory decision when the cause of the quarrel was submitted to arbitration.

Two Footpads

Two Footpads sat at their grog in a roadside resort, comparing the evening's adventures.

"I stood up the Chief of Police," said the First Footpad, "and I got away with what he had."

"And I," said the Second Footpad, "stood up the United States District Attorney, and got away with——"

"Good Lord!" interrupted the other in astonishment and admiration—"you got away with what that fellow had?"

"No," the unfortunate narrator explained—"with a small part of what *I* had."

Equipped for Service

During the Civil War a Patriot was passing through the State of Maryland with a pass from the President to join Grant's army and see the fighting. Stopping a day at Annapolis, he visited the shop of a well-known optician and ordered seven powerful telescopes, one for every day in the week. In recognition of this munificent patronage of the State's languishing industries, the Governor commissioned him a colonel.

The Basking Cyclone

A Negro in a boat, gathering driftwood, saw a sleeping Alligator, and, thinking it was a log, fell to estimating the number of shingles it would make for his new cabin. Having satisfied his mind on that point, he stuck his boat-hook into the beast's back to harvest his good fortune. Thereupon the saurian emerged from his dream and took to the water, greatly to the surprise of the man-and-brother.

"I never befo' seen such a cyclone as dat," he exclaimed as soon as he had recovered his breath. "It done carry away de ruf of my house!"

At the Pole

After a great expenditure of life and treasure a Daring Explorer had succeeded in reaching the North Pole, when he was approached by a Native Galeut who lived there.

"Good morning," said the Native Galeut. "I'm very glad to see you, but why did you come here?"

"Glory," said the Daring Explorer, curtly.

"Yes, yes, I know," the other persisted; "but of what benefit to man is your discovery? To what truths does it give access which were inaccessible before?—facts, I mean, having a scientific value?"

"I'll be Tom scatted if I know," the great man replied, frankly; "you will have to ask the Scientist of the Expedition."

But the Scientist of the Expedition explained that he had been so engrossed with the care of his instruments and the study of his tables that he had found no time to think of it.

The Optimist and the Cynic

A man who had experienced the favours of fortune and was an Optimist, met a man who had experienced an optimist and was a Cynic. So the Cynic turned out of the road to let the Optimist roll by in his gold carriage.

"My son," said the Optimist, stopping the gold carriage, "you look as if you had not a friend in the world."

"I don't know if I have or not," replied the Cynic, "for you have the world."

The Poet and the Editor

"My dear sir," said the editor to the man who had called to see about his poem, "I regret to say that owing to an unfortunate altercation in this office the greater part of your manuscript is illegible; a bottle of ink was upset upon it, blotting out all but the first line—that is to say—

The autumn leaves were falling, falling.

"Unluckily, not having read the poem, I was unable to supply the incidents that followed; otherwise we could have given them in our own words. If the news is not stale, and has not already appeared in the other papers, perhaps you will kindly relate what occurred, while I make notes of it.

The autumn leaves were falling, falling.

"Go on."

"What!" said the poet, "do you expect me to reproduce the entire poem from memory?"

"Only the substance of it—just the leading facts. We will add whatever is necessary in the way of amplification and embellishment. It will detain you but a moment.

The autumn leaves were falling, falling——

"Now, then."

There was a sound of a slow getting up and going away. The chronicler of passing events sat through it, motionless, with suspended pen; and when the movement was complete Poesy was represented in that place by nothing but a warm spot on the wooden chair.

The Taken Hand

A Successful Man of Business, having occasion to write to a Thief, expressed a wish to see him and shake hands.

"No," replied the Thief, "there are some things which I will not take—among them your hand."

"You must use a little strategy," said a Philosopher to whom the Successful Man of Business had reported the Thief's haughty reply. "Leave your hand out some night, and he will take it."

So one night the Successful Man of Business left his hand out of his neighbour's pocket, and the Thief took it with avidity.

An Unspeakable Imbecile

A Judge said to a Convicted Assassin:

"Prisoner at the bar, have you anything to say why the death-sentence should not be passed upon you?"

"Will what I say make any difference?" asked the Convicted Assassin.

"I do not see how it can," the Judge answered, reflectively. "No, it will not."

"Then," said the doomed one, "I should just like to remark that you are the most unspeakable old imbecile in seven States and the District of Columbia."

A Needful War

The people of Madagonia had an antipathy to the people of Novakatka and set upon some sailors of a Novakatkan vessel, killing two and wounding twelve. The King of Madagonia having refused either to apologise or pay, the King of Novakatka made war upon him, saying that it was necessary to show that Novakatkans must not be slaughtered. In the battles which ensued the people of Madagonia slaughtered two thousand Novakatkans and wounded twelve thousand. But the Madagonians were unsuccessful, which so chagrined them that never thereafter in all their land was a Novakatkan secure in property or life.

The Mine Owner and the Jackass

While the Owner of a Silver Mine was on his way to attend a convention of his species he was accosted by a Jackass, who said:

"By an unjust discrimination against quadrupeds I am made ineligible to a seat in your convention; so I am compelled to seek representation through you."

"It will give me great pleasure, sir," said the Owner of a Silver Mine, "to serve one so closely allied to me in—in—well, you know," he added, with a significant gesture of his two hands upward from the sides of his head. "What do you want?"

"Oh, nothing—nothing at all for myself individually," replied the Donkey; "but his country's welfare should be a patriot's supreme care. If Americans are to retain the sacred liberties for which their fathers strove, Congress must declare our independence of European dictation by maintaining the price of mules."

The Dog and the Physician

A Dog that had seen a Physician attending the burial of a wealthy patient, said: "When do you expect to dig it up?"

"Why should I dig it up?" the Physician asked.

"When I bury a bone," said the Dog, "it is with an intention to uncover it later and pick it."

"The bones that I bury," said the Physician, "are those that I can no longer pick."

The Party Manager and the Gentleman

A Party Manager said to a Gentleman whom he saw minding his own business:

"How much will you pay for a nomination to office?"

"Nothing," the Gentleman replied.

"But you will contribute something to the campaign fund to assist in your election, will you not?" asked the Party Manager, winking.

"Oh, no," said the Gentleman, gravely. "If the people wish me to work for them, they must hire me without solicitation. I am very comfortable without office."

"But," urged the Party Manager, "an election is a thing to be desired. It is a high honour to be a servant of the people."

"If servitude is a high honour," the Gentleman said, "it would be indecent for me to seek it; and if obtained by my own exertion it would be no honour."

"Well," persisted the Party Manager, "you will at least, I hope, indorse the party platform."

The Gentleman replied: "It is improbable that its authors have accurately expressed my views without consulting me; and if I indorsed their work without approving it I should be a liar."

"You are a detestable hypocrite and an idiot!" shouted the Party Manager.

"Even your good opinion of my fitness," replied the Gentleman, "shall not persuade me."

The Legislator and the Citizen

An ex-Legislator asked a Most Respectable Citizen for a letter to the Governor recommending him for appointment as Commissioner of Shrimps and Crabs.

"Sir," said the Most Respectable Citizen, austerely, "were you not once in the State Senate?"

"Not so bad as that, sir, I assure you," was the reply. "I was a member of the Slower House. I was expelled for selling my influence for money."

"And you dare to ask for mine!" shouted the Most Respectable Citizen. "You have the impudence? A man who will accept bribes will probably offer them. Do you mean to——"

"I should not think of making a corrupt proposal to you, sir; but if I were Commissioner of Shrimps and Crabs, I might have some influence with the waterfront population, and be able to help you make your fight for Coroner."

"In that case I do not feel justified in denying you the letter."

So he took his pen, and, some demon guiding his hand, he wrote, greatly to his astonishment:

> *Who sells his influence should stop it,*
> *An honest man will only swap it.*

The Rainmaker

An Officer of the Government, with a great outfit of mule-waggons loaded with balloons, kites, dynamite bombs, and electrical apparatus, halted in the midst of a desert, where there had been no rain for ten years, and set up a camp. After several months of preparation and an expenditure of a million dollars all was in readiness, and a series of tremendous explosions occurred on the earth and in the sky. This was followed by a great downpour of rain, which washed the unfortunate Officer of the Government and the outfit off the face of creation and affected the agricultural heart with joy too deep for utterance. A Newspaper Reporter who had just arrived escaped by climbing a hill near by, and there he found the Sole Survivor of the expedition—a mule-driver—down on his knees behind a mesquite bush, praying with extreme fervour.

"Oh, you can't stop it that way," said the Reporter.

"My fellow-traveller to the bar of God," replied the Sole Survivor, looking up over his shoulder, "your understanding is in darkness. I am not stopping this great blessing; under Providence, I am bringing it."

"That is a pretty good joke," said the Reporter, laughing as well as he could in the strangling rain—"a mule driver's prayer answered!"

"Child of levity and scoffing," replied the other; "you err again, misled by these humble habiliments. I am the Rev. Ezekiel Thrifft, a minister of the gospel, now in the service of the great manufacturing firm of Skinn & Sheer. They make balloons, kites, dynamite bombs, and electrical apparatus."

The Citizen and the Snakes

A Public-spirited Citizen who had failed miserably in trying to secure a National political convention for his city suffered acutely from dejection. While in that frame of mind he leaned thoughtlessly against a druggist's show-window, wherein were one hundred and fifty kinds of assorted snakes. The glass breaking, the reptiles all escaped into the street.

"When you can't do what you wish," said the Public-spirited Citizen, "it is worth while to do what you can."

Fortune and the Fabulist

A Writer of Fables was passing through a lonely forest when he met a Fortune. Greatly alarmed, he tried to climb a tree, but the Fortune pulled him down and bestowed itself upon him with cruel persistence.

"Why did you try to run away?" said the Fortune, when his struggles had ceased and his screams were stilled. "Why do you glare at me so inhospitably?"

"I don't know what you are," replied the Writer of Fables, deeply disturbed.

"I am wealth; I am respectability," the Fortune explained; "I am elegant houses, a yacht, and a clean shirt every day. I am leisure, I am travel, wine, a shiny hat, and an unshiny coat. I am enough to eat."

"All right," said the Writer of Fables, in a whisper; "but for goodness' sake speak lower."

"Why so?" the Fortune asked, in surprise.

"So as not to wake me," replied the Writer of Fables, a holy calm brooding upon his beautiful face.

A Smiling Idol

An Idol said to a Missionary, "My friend, why do you seek to bring me into contempt? If it had not been for me, what would you have been? Remember thy creator that thy days be long in the land."

"I confess," replied the Missionary, fingering a number of ten-cent pieces which a Sunday-school in his own country had forwarded to him, "that I am a product of you, but I protest that you cannot quote Scripture with accuracy and point. Therefore will I continue to go up against you with the Sword of the Spirit."

Shortly afterwards the Idol's worshippers held a great religious ceremony at the base of his pedestal, and as a part of the rites the Missionary was roasted whole. As the tongue was removed for the high priest's table, "Ah," said the Idol to himself, "that is the Sword of the Spirit—the only Sword that is less dangerous when unsheathed."

And he smiled so pleasantly at his own wit that the provinces of Ghargaroo, M'gwana, and Scowow were affected with a blight.

Philosophers Three

A Bear, a Fox, and an Opossum were attacked by an inundation.

"Death loves a coward," said the Bear, and went forward to fight the flood.

"What a fool!" said the Fox. "I know a trick worth two of that." And he slipped into a hollow stump.

"There are malevolent forces," said the Opossum, "which the wise will neither confront nor avoid. The thing is to know the nature of your antagonist."

So saying the Opossum lay down and pretended to be dead.

The Boneless King

Some Apes who had deposed their king fell at once into dissension and anarchy. In this strait they sent a Deputation to a neighbouring tribe to consult the Oldest and Wisest Ape in All the World.

"My children," said the Oldest and Wisest Ape in All the World, when he had heard the Deputation, "you did right in ridding yourselves of tyranny, but your tribe is not sufficiently advanced to dispense with the forms of monarchy. Entice the tyrant back with fair promises, kill him and enthrone. The skeleton of even the most lawless despot makes a good constitutional sovereign."

At this the Deputation was greatly abashed. "It is impossible," they said, moving away; "our king has no skeleton; he was stuffed."

Uncalculating Zeal

A man-eating tiger was ravaging the Kingdom of Damnasia, and the King, greatly concerned for the lives and limbs of his Royal subjects, promised his daughter Zodroulra to any man who would kill the animal. After some days Camaraladdin appeared before the King and claimed the reward.

"But where is the tiger?" the King asked.

"May jackasses sing above my uncle's grave," replied Camaraladdin, "if I dared go within a league of him!"

"Wretch!" cried the King, unsheathing his consoler-under-disappointment; "how dare you claim my daughter when you have done nothing to earn her?"

"Thou art wiser, O King, than Solyman the Great, and thy servant is as dust in the tomb of thy dog, yet thou errest. I did not, it is true, kill the tiger, but behold! I have brought thee the scalp of the man who had accumulated five million pieces of gold and was after more."

The King drew his consoler-under-disappointment, and, flicking off Camaraladdin's head, said:

"Learn, caitiff, the expediency of uncalculating zeal. If the millionaire had been let alone he would have devoured the tiger."

A Transposition

Travelling through the sage-brush country a Jackass met a rabbit, who exclaimed in great astonishment:

"Good heavens! how did you grow so big? You are doubtless the largest rabbit living."

"No," said the Jackass, "you are the smallest donkey."

After a good deal of fruitless argument the question was referred for decision to a passing Coyote, who was a bit of a demagogue and desirous to stand well with both.

"Gentlemen," said he, "you are both right, as was to have been expected by persons so gifted with appliances for receiving instruction from the wise. You, sir,"—turning to the superior animal—"are, as he has accurately observed, a rabbit. And you"—to the other—"are correctly described as a jackass. In transposing your names man has acted with incredible folly."

They were so pleased with the decision that they declared the Coyote their candidate for the Grizzly Bearship; but whether he ever obtained the office history does not relate.

The Honest Citizen

A Political Preferment, labelled with its price, was canvassing the State to find a purchaser. One day it offered itself to a Truly Good Man, who, after examining the label and finding the price was exactly twice as great as he was willing to pay, spurned the Political Preferment from his door. Then the People said: "Behold, this is an honest citizen!" And the Truly Good Man humbly confessed that it was so.

A Creaking Tail

An American Statesman who had twisted the tail of the British Lion until his arms ached was at last rewarded by a sharp, rasping sound.

"I knew your fortitude would give out after a while," said the American Statesman, delighted; "your agony attests my political power."

"Agony I know not!" said the British Lion, yawning: "the swivel in my tail needs a few drops of oil, that is all."

Wasted Sweets

A Candidate canvassing his district met a Nurse wheeling a Baby in a carriage, and, stooping, imprinted a kiss upon the Baby's clammy muzzle. Rising, he saw a Man, who laughed.

"Why do you laugh?" asked the Candidate.

"Because," replied the Man, "the Baby belongs to the Orphan Asylum."

"But the Nurse," said the Candidate—"the Nurse will surely relate the touching incident wherever she goes, and perhaps write to her former master."

"The Nurse," said the Man who had laughed, "is an inmate of the Institution for the Illiterate-Deaf-and-Dumb."

Six and One

The Committee on Gerrymander worked late, drawing intricate lines on a map of the State, and being weary sought repose in a game of poker. At the close of the game the six Republican members were bankrupt and the single Democrat had all the money. On the next day, when the Committee was called to order for business, one of the luckless six mounted his legs, and said:

"Mr. Chairman, before we bend to our noble task of purifying politics, in the interest of good government I wish to say a word of the untoward events of last evening. If my memory serves me the disasters which overtook the Majority of this honourable body always befell when it was the Minority's deal. It is my solemn conviction, Mr. Chairman, and to its affirmation I pledge my life, my fortune, and my sacred honour, that that wicked and unscrupulous Minority redistricted the cards!"

The Sportsman and the Squirrel

A Sportsman who had wounded a Squirrel, which was making desperate efforts to drag itself away, ran after it with a stick, exclaiming:

"Poor thing! I will put it out of its misery."

At that moment the Squirrel stopped from exhaustion, and looking up at its enemy, said:

"I don't venture to doubt the sincerity of your compassion, though it comes rather late, but you seem to lack the faculty of observation. Do you not perceive by my actions that the dearest wish of my heart is to continue in my misery?"

At this exposure of his hypocrisy, the Sportsman was so overcome with shame and remorse that he would not strike the Squirrel, but pointing it out to his dog, walked thoughtfully away.

The Fogy and the Sheik

A Fogy who lived in a cave near a great caravan route returned to his home one day and saw, near by, a great concourse of men and animals, and in their midst a tower, at the foot of which something with wheels smoked and panted like an exhausted horse. He sought the Sheik of the Outfit.

"What sin art thou committing now, O son of a Christian dog?" said the Fogy, with a truly Oriental politeness.

"Boring for water, you black-and-tan galoot!" replied the Sheik of the Outfit, with that ready repartee which distinguishes the Unbeliever.

"Knowest thou not, thou whelp of darkness and father of disordered livers," cried the Fogy, "that water will cause grass to spring up here, and trees, and possibly even flowers? Knowest thou not, that thou art, in truth, producing an oasis?"

"And don't you know," said the Sheik of the Outfit, "that caravans will then stop here for rest and refreshments, giving you a chance to steal the camels, the horses, and the goods?"

"May the wild hog defile my grave, but thou speakest wisdom!" the Fogy replied, with the dignity of his race, extending his hand. "Sheik."

They shook.

At Heaven's Gate

Having arisen from the tomb, a Woman presented herself at the gate of Heaven, and knocked with a trembling hand.

"Madam," said Saint Peter, rising and approaching the wicket, "whence do you come?"

"From San Francisco," replied the Woman, with embarrassment, as great beads of perspiration spangled her spiritual brow.

"Never mind, my good girl," the Saint said, compassionately. "Eternity is a long time; you can live that down."

"But that, if you please, is not all." The Woman was growing more and more confused. "I poisoned my husband. I chopped up my babies. I——"

"Ah," said the Saint, with sudden austerity, "your confession suggests a very grave possibility. Were you a member of the Women's Press Association?"

The lady drew herself up and replied with warmth:

"I was not."

The gates of pearl and jasper swung back upon their golden hinges, making the most ravishing music, and the Saint, stepping aside, bowed low, saying:

"Enter, then, into thine eternal rest."

But the Woman hesitated.

"The poisoning—the chopping—the—the—" she stammered.

"Of no consequence, I assure you. We are not going to be hard on a lady who did not belong to the Women's Press Association. Take a harp."

"But I applied for membership—I was blackballed."

"Take two harps."

The Catted Anarchist

An Anarchist Orator who had been struck in the face with a Dead Cat by some Respector of Law to him unknown, had the Dead Cat arrested and taken before a Magistrate.

"Why do you appeal to the law?" said the Magistrate—"You who go in for the abolition of law."

"That," replied the Anarchist, who was not without a certain hardness of head, "that is none of your business; I am not bound to be consistent. You sit here to do justice between me and this Dead Cat."

"Very well," said the Magistrate, putting on the black cap and a solemn look; "as the accused makes no defence, and is undoubtedly guilty, I sentence her to be eaten by the public executioner; and as that position happens to be vacant, I appoint you to it, without bonds."

One of the most delighted spectators at the execution was the anonymous Respector of Law who had flung the condemned.

The Honourable Member

A member of a Legislature, who had pledged himself to his Constituents not to steal, brought home at the end of the session a large part of the dome of the Capitol. Thereupon the Constituents held an indignation meeting and passed a resolution of tar and feathers.

"You are most unjust," said the Member of the Legislature. "It is true I promised you I would not steal; but had I ever promised you that I would not lie?"

The Constituents said he was an honourable man and elected him to the United States Congress, unpledged and unfledged.

The Expatriated Boss

A Boss who had gone to Canada was taunted by a Citizen of Montreal with having fled to avoid prosecution.

"You do me a grave injustice," said the Boss, parting with a pair of tears. "I came to Canada solely because of its political attractions; its Government is the most corrupt in the world."

"Pray forgive me," said the Citizen of Montreal.

They fell upon each other's neck, and at the conclusion of that touching rite the Boss had two watches.

An Inadequate Fee

An Ox, unable to extricate himself from the mire into which he sank, was advised to make use of a Political Pull. When the Political Pull had arrived, the Ox said: "My good friend, please make fast to me, and let nature take her course."

So the Political Pull made fast to the Ox's head and nature took her course. The Ox was drawn, first, from the mire, and, next, from his skin. Then the Political Pull looked back upon the good fat carcase of beef that he was dragging to his lair and said, with a discontented spirit:

"That is hardly my customary fee; I'll take home this first instalment, then return and bring an action for salvage against the skin."

The Judge and the Plaintiff

A Man of Experience in Business was awaiting the judgment of the Court in an action for damages which he had brought against a railway company. The door opened and the Judge of the Court entered.

"Well," said he, "I am going to decide your case to-day. If I should decide in your favour, I wonder how you would express your satisfaction?"

"Sir," said the Man of Experience in Business, "I should risk your anger by offering you one half the sum awarded."

"Did I say I was going to decide that case?" said the Judge, abruptly, as if awakening from a dream. "Dear me, how absent-minded I am. I mean I have already decided it, and judgment has been entered for the full amount that you sued for."

"Did I say I would give you one half?" said the Man of Experience in Business, coldly. "Dear me, how near I came to being a rascal. I mean, that I am greatly obliged to you."

The Return of the Representative

Hearing that the Legislature had adjourned, the people of an Assembly District held a mass-meeting to devise a suitable punishment for their representative. By one speaker it was proposed that he be disembowelled, by another that he be made to run the gauntlet. Some favoured hanging, some thought that it would do him good to appear in a suit of tar and feathers. An old man, famous for his wisdom and his habit of drooling on his shirt-front, suggested that they first catch their hare. So the Chairman appointed a committee to watch for the victim at midnight, and take him as he should attempt to sneak into town across-lots from the tamarack swamp. At this point in the proceedings they were interrupted by the sound of a brass band. Their dishonoured representative was driving up from the railway station in a coach-and-four, with music and a banner. A few moments later he entered the hall, went upon the platform, and said it was the proudest moment of his life. (Cheers.)

A Statesman

A Statesman who attended a meeting of a Chamber of Commerce rose to speak, but was objected to on the ground that he had nothing to do with commerce.

"Mr. Chairman," said an Aged Member, rising, "I conceive that the objection is not well taken; the gentleman's connection with commerce is close and intimate. He is a Commodity."

Two Dogs

The Dog, as created, had a rigid tail, but after some centuries of a cheerless existence, unappreciated by Man, who made him work for his living, he implored the Creator to endow him with a wag. This being done he was able to dissemble his resentment with a sign of affection, and the earth was his and the fulness thereof. Observing this, the Politician (an animal created later) petitioned that a wag might be given him too. As he was incaudate it was conferred upon his chin, which he now wags with great profit and gratification except when he is at his meals.

Three Recruits

A Farmer, an Artisan, and a Labourer went to the King of their country and complained that they were compelled to support a large standing army of mere consumers, who did nothing for their keep.

"Very well," said the King, "my subjects' wishes are the highest law."

So he disbanded his army and the consumers became producers also. The sale of their products so brought down prices that farming was ruined, and their skilled and unskilled labour drove the artisans and labourers into the almshouses and highways. In a few years the national distress was so great that the Farmer, the Artisan, and the Labourer petitioned the King to reorganize the standing army.

"What!" said the King; "you wish to support those idle consumers again?"

"No, your Majesty," they replied— "we wish to enlist."

The Mirror

A silken-eared Spaniel, who traced his descent from King Charles the Second of England, chanced to look into a mirror which was leaning against the wainscoting of a room on the ground floor of his mistress's house. Seeing his reflection, he supposed it to be another dog, outside, and said:

"I can chew up any such milksoppy pup as that, and I will."

So he ran out-of-doors and around to the side of the house where he fancied the enemy was. It so happened that at that moment a Bulldog sat there sunning his teeth. The Spaniel stopped short in dire consternation, and, after regarding the Bulldog a moment from a safe distance, said:

"I don't know whether you cultivate the arts of peace or your flag is flung to the battle and the breeze and your voice is for war. If you are a civilian, the windows of this house flatter you worse than a newspaper, but if you're a soldier, they do you a grave injustice."

This speech being unintelligible to the Bulldog he only civilly smiled, which so terrified the Spaniel that he dropped dead in his tracks.

Saint and Sinner

"My friend," said a distinguished officer of the Salvation Army, to a Most Wicked Sinner, "I was once a drunkard, a thief, an assassin. The Divine Grace has made me what I am."

The Most Wicked Sinner looked at him from head to foot. "Henceforth," he said, "the Divine Grace, I fancy, will let well enough alone."

An Antidote

A Young Ostrich came to its Mother, groaning with pain and with its wings tightly crossed upon its stomach.

"What have you been eating?" the Mother asked, with solicitude.

"Nothing but a keg of Nails," was the reply.

"What!" exclaimed the Mother; "a whole keg of Nails, at your age! Why, you will kill yourself that way. Go quickly, my child, and swallow a claw-hammer."

A Weary Echo

A Convention of female writers, which for two days had been stuffing Woman's couch with goose-quills and hailing the down of a new era, adjourned with unabated enthusiasm, shouting, "Place aux dames!" And Echo wearily replied, "Oh, damn."

The Ingenious Blackmailer

An Inventor went to a King and was granted an audience, when the following conversation ensued:

Inventor—"May it please your Majesty, I have invented a rifle that discharges lightning."

King—"Ah, you wish to sell me the secret."

Inventor—"Yes; it will enable your army to overrun any nation that is accessible."

King—"In order to get any good of my outlay for your invention, I must make a war, and do so as soon as I can arm my troops—before your secret is discovered by foreign nations. How much do you want?"

Inventor—"One million dollars."

King—"And how much will it cost to make the change of arms?"

Inventor—"Fifty millions."

King—"And the war will cost——?"

Inventor—"But consider the glory and the spoils!"

King—"Exactly. But if I am not seeking these advantages? What if I decline to purchase?"

Inventor—"There is no economy in that. Though a patriot, I am poor; if my own country will not patronise me, I must seek a market elsewhere."

King (to Prime Minister)—"Take this blackmailer and cut off his head."

A Talisman

Having been summoned to serve as a juror, a Prominent Citizen sent a physician's certificate stating that he was afflicted with softening of the brain.

"The gentleman is excused," said the Judge, handing back the certificate to the person who had brought it, "he has a brain."

The Ancient Order

Hardly had that ancient order, the Sultans of Exceeding Splendour, been completely founded by the Grand Flashing Inaccessible, when a question arose as to what should be the title of address among the members. Some wanted it to be

simply "my Lord," others held out for "your Dukeness," and
still others preferred "my Sovereign Liege." Finally the gorgeous jewel of the order, gleaming upon the breast of every
member, suggested "your Badgesty," which was adopted,
and the order became popularly known as the Kings of
Catarrh.

A Fatal Disorder

A Dying Man who had been shot was requested by officers
of the law to make a statement, and be quick about it.

"You were assaulted without provocation, of course," said
the District Attorney, preparing to set down the answer.

"No," replied the Dying Man, "I was the aggressor."

"Yes, I understand," said the District Attorney; "you
committed the aggression—you were compelled to, as it were.
You did it in self-defence."

"I don't think he would have hurt me if I had let him
alone," said the other. "No, I fancy he was a man of peace
and would not have hurt a fly. I brought such a pressure to
bear on him that he naturally had to yield—he couldn't hold
out. If he had refused to shoot me I don't see how I could
decently have continued his acquaintance."

"Good Heavens!" exclaimed the District Attorney, throw-
ing down his notebook and pencil; "this is all quite irregular.
I can't make use of such an ante-mortem statement as that."

"I never before knew a man to tell the truth," said the
Chief of Police, "when dying of violence."

"Violence nothing!" the Police Surgeon said, pulling out
and inspecting the man's tongue—"it is the truth that is
killing him."

The Massacre

Some Holy Missionaries in China having been deprived of
life by the Bigoted Heathens, the Christian Press made a note

of it, and was greatly pained to point out the contrast between the Bigoted Heathens and the law-abiding countrymen of the Holy Missionaries who had wickedly been sent to eternal bliss.

"Yes," assented a Miserable Sinner, as he finished reading the articles, "the Heathens of Ying Shing are deceitful above all things and desperately wicked. By the way," he added, turning over the paper to read the entertaining and instructive Fables, "I know the Heathenese lingo. Ying Shing means Rock Creek; it is in the Province of Wyo Ming."

A Ship and a Man

Seeing a ship sailing by upon the sea of politics, an Ambitious Person started in hot pursuit along the strand; but the people's eyes being fixed upon the Presidency no one observed the pursuer. This greatly annoyed him, and recollecting that he was not aquatic, he stopped and shouted across the waves' tumultuous roar:

"Take my name off the passenger list."

Back to him over the waters, hollow and heartless, like laughter in a tomb, rang the voice of the Skipper:

"'Tain't on!"

And there, in the focus of a million pairs of convergent eyes, the Ambitious Person sat him down between the sun and moon and murmured sadly to his own soul:

"Marooned, by thunder!"

Congress and the People

Successive Congresses having greatly impoverished the People, they were discouraged and wept copiously.

"Why do you weep?" inquired an Angel who had perched upon a fence near by.

"They have taken all we have," replied the People—
"excepting," they added, noting the suggestive visitant
—"excepting our hope in Heaven. Thank God, they cannot
deprive us of that!"

But at last came the Congress of 1889.

The Justice and His Accuser

An eminent Justice of the Supreme Court of Patagascar
was accused of having obtained his appointment by fraud.

"You wander," he said to the Accuser; "it is of little importance how I obtained my power; it is only important how
I have used it."

"I confess," said the Accuser, "that in comparison with the
rascally way in which you have conducted yourself on the
Bench, the rascally way in which you got there does seem
rather a trifle."

The Highwayman and the Traveller

A Highwayman confronted a Traveller, and covering him
with a firearm, shouted: "Your money or your life!"

"My good friend," said the Traveller, "according to the
terms of your demand my money will save my life, my life my
money; you imply you will take one or the other, but not
both. If that is what you mean, please be good enough to take
my life."

"That is not what I mean," said the Highwayman; "you
cannot save your money by giving up your life."

"Then take it, anyhow," the Traveller said. "If it will not
save my money, it is good for nothing."

The Highwayman was so pleased with the Traveller's
philosophy and wit that he took him into partnership, and
this splendid combination of talent started a newspaper.

The Policeman and the Citizen

A Policeman, finding a man that had fallen in a fit, said, "This man is drunk," and began beating him on the head with his club. A passing Citizen said:

"Why do you murder a man that is already harmless?"

Thereupon the Policeman left the man in a fit and attacked the Citizen, who, after receiving several severe contusions, ran away.

"Alas," said the Policeman, "why did I not attack the sober one before exhausting myself upon the other?"

Thenceforward he pursued that plan, and by zeal and diligence rose to be Chief, and sobriety is unknown in the region subject to his sway.

The Writer and the Tramps

An Ambitious Writer, distinguished for the condition of his linen, was travelling the high road to fame, when he met a Tramp.

"What is the matter with your shirt?" inquired the Tramp.

"It bears the marks of that superb unconcern which is the characteristic of genius," replied the Ambitious Writer, contemptuously passing him by.

Resting by the wayside a little later, the Tramp carved upon the smooth bark of a birch-tree the words, "John Gump, Champion Genius."

Two Politicians

Two Politicians were exchanging ideas regarding the rewards for public service.

"The reward which I most desire," said the First Politician, "is the gratitude of my fellow-citizens."

"That would be very gratifying, no doubt," said the Second Politician, "but, alas! in order to obtain it one has to retire from politics."

For an instant they gazed upon each other with inexpressible tenderness; then the First Politician murmured, "God's will be done! Since we cannot hope for reward, let us be content with what we have."

And lifting their right hands from the public treasury they swore to be content.

The Fugitive Office

A Traveller arriving at the capitol of the nation saw a vast plain outside the wall, filled with struggling and shouting men. While he looked upon the alarming spectacle an Office broke away from the Throng and took shelter in a tomb close to where he stood, the crowd being too intent upon hammering one another to observe that the cause of their contention had departed.

"Poor bruised and bleeding creature," said the compassionate Traveller, "what misfortune caused you to be so far away from the source of power?"

"I 'sought the man,'" said the Office.

The Tyrant Frog

A Snake swallowing a frog head-first was approached by a Naturalist with a stick.

"Ah, my deliverer," said the Snake as well as he could, "you have arrived just in time; this reptile, you see, is pitching into me without provocation."

"Sir," replied the Naturalist, "I need a snakeskin for my collection, but if you had not explained I should not have interrupted you, for I thought you were at dinner."

The Eligible Son-in-Law

A Truly Pious Person who conducted a savings bank and lent money to his sisters and his cousins and his aunts of both sexes, was approached by a Tatterdemalion, who applied for a loan of one hundred thousand dollars.

"What security have you to offer?" asked the Truly Pious Person.

"The best in the world," the applicant replied, confidentially; "I am about to become your son-in-law."

"That would indeed be gilt-edged," said the banker, gravely; "but what claim have you to the hand of my daughter?"

"One that cannot be lightly denied," said the Tatterdemalion. "I am about to become worth one hundred thousand dollars."

Unable to detect a weak point in this scheme of mutual advantage, the financier gave the promoter in disguise an order for the money, and wrote a note to his wife directing her to count out the girl.

The Statesman and the Horse

A Statesman who had saved his country was returning from Washington on foot, when he met a Race Horse going at full speed, and stopped it.

"Turn about and travel the other way," said the Statesman, "and I will keep you company as far as my home. The advantages of travelling together are obvious."

"I cannot do that," said the Race Horse; "I am following my master to Washington. I did not go fast enough to suit him, and he has gone on ahead."

"Who is your master?" inquired the Statesman.

"He is the Statesman who saved his country," answered the Race Horse.

"There appears to be some mistake," the other said. "Why did he wish to travel so fast?"

"So as to be there in time to get the country that he saved."

"I guess he got it," said the other, and limped along, sighing.

An Ærophobe

A Celebrated Divine having affirmed the fallibility of the Bible, was asked why, then, he preached the religion founded upon it.

"If it is fallible," he replied, "there is the greater reason that I explain it, lest it mislead."

"Then am I to infer," said his Questioner, "that *you* are not fallible?"

"You are to infer that I am not pneumophagous."

The Thrift of Strength

A Weak Man going down-hill met a Strong Man going up, and said:

"I take this direction because it requires less exertion, not from choice. I pray you, sir, assist me to regain the summit."

"Gladly," said the Strong Man, his face illuminated with the glory of the thought. "I have always considered my strength a sacred gift in trust for my fellow-men. I will take you along with me. Just get behind me and push."

The Good Government

"What a happy land you are!" said a Republican Form of Government to a Sovereign State. "Be good enough to lie still while I walk upon you, singing the praises of universal suffrage and descanting upon the blessings of civil and religious liberty. In the meantime you can relieve your feelings by cursing the one-man power and the effete monarchies of Europe."

"My public servants have been fools and rogues from the date of your accession to power," replied the State; "my legislative bodies, both State and municipal, are bands of thieves; my taxes are insupportable; my courts are corrupt; my cities are a disgrace to civilisation; my corporations have their hands at the throats of every private interest—all my affairs are in disorder and criminal confusion."

"That is all very true," said the Republican Form of Government, putting on its hobnail shoes; "but consider how I thrill you every Fourth of July."

The Life-Saver

An Ancient Maiden, standing on the edge of a wharf near a Modern Swain, was overheard rehearsing the words:

"Noble preserver! The life that you have saved is yours!"

Having repeated them several times with various intonations, she sprang into the water, where she was suffered to drown.

"I am a noble preserver," said the Modern Swain, thoughtfully moving away; "the life that I have saved is indeed mine."

The Man and the Bird

A Man with a Shotgun said to a Bird:

"It is all nonsense, you know, about shooting being a cruel sport. I put my skill against your cunning—that is all there is of it. It is a fair game."

"True," said the Bird, "but I don't wish to play."

"Why not?" inquired the Man with a Shotgun.

"The game," the Bird replied, "is fair as you say; the chances are about even; but consider the stake. I am in it for you, but what is there in it for me?"

Not being prepared with an answer to the question, the Man with a Shotgun sagaciously removed the propounder.

From the Minutes

An Orator afflicted with atrophy of the organ of common-sense rose in his place in the halls of legislation and pointed with pride to his Unblotted Escutcheon. Seeing what it supposed to be the finger of scorn pointed at it, the Unblotted Escutcheon turned black with rage. Seeing the Unblotted Escutcheon turning black with what he supposed to be the record of his own misdeeds showing through the whitewash, the Orator fell dead of mortification. Seeing the Orator fall dead of what they supposed to be atrophy of the organ of common-sense, his colleagues resolved that whenever they should adjourn because they were tired, it should be out of respect to the memory of him who had so frequently made them so.

Three of a Kind

A Lawyer in whom an instinct of justice had survived the wreck of his ignorance of law was retained for the defence of a burglar whom the police had taken after a desperate struggle with someone not in custody. In consultation with his client the Lawyer asked, "Have you accomplices?"

"Yes, sir," replied the Burglar. "I have two, but neither has been taken. I hired one to defend me against capture, you to defend me against conviction."

This answer deeply impressed the Lawyer, and having ascertained that the Burglar had accumulated no money in his profession he threw up the case.

The Fabulist and the Animals

A wise and illustrious Writer of Fables was visiting a travelling menagerie with a view to collecting literary materials. As he was passing near the Elephant, that animal said:

"How sad that so justly famous a satirist should mar his work by ridicule of people with long noses—who are the salt of the earth!"

The Kangaroo said:

"I do so enjoy that great man's censure of the ridiculous—particularly his attacks on the Proboscidæ; but, alas! he has no reverence for the Marsupials, and laughs at our way of carrying our young in a pouch."

The Camel said:

"If he would only respect the sacred Hump, he would be faultless. As it is, I cannot permit his fables to be read in the presence of my family."

The Ostrich, seeing his approach, thrust her head in the straw, saying:

"If I do not conceal myself, he may be reminded to write something disagreeable about my lack of a crest or my appetite for scrap-iron; and although he is inexpressibly brilliant when he devotes himself to censure of folly and greed, his dulness is matchless when he transcends the limits of legitimate comment."

"That," said the Buzzard to his mate, "is the distinguished author of that glorious fable, 'The Ostrich and the Keg of Raw Nails.' I regret to add, that he wrote, also, 'The Buzzard's Feast,' in which a carrion diet is contumeliously disparaged. A carrion diet is the foundation of sound health. If nothing else but corpses were eaten, death would be unknown."

Seeing an attendant approaching, the wise and illustrious Writer of Fables passed out of the tent and mingled with the crowd. It was afterward discovered that he had crept in under the canvas without paying.

A Revivalist Revived

A Revivalist who had fallen dead in the pulpit from too violent religious exercise was astonished to wake up in Hades. He promptly sent for the Adversary of Souls and demanded his freedom, explaining that he was entirely orthodox, and had always led a pious and holy life.

"That is all very true," said the Adversary, "but you taught by example that a verb should not agree with its subject in person and number, whereas the Good Book says that contention is worse than a dinner of herbs. You also tried to release the objective case from its thraldom to the preposition, and it is written that servants should obey their masters. You stay right here."

The Debaters

A Hurled-back Allegation, which, after a brief rest, had again started forth upon its mission of mischief, met an Inkstand in mid-air.

"How did the Honourable Member whom you represent know that I was coming again?" inquired the Hurled-back Allegation.

"He did not," the Inkstand replied; "he isn't at all forehanded at repartee."

"Why, then, do you come, things being even when he had hurled me back?"

"He wanted to be a little ahead."

Two of the Pious

A Christian and a Heathen in His Blindness were disputing, when the Christian, with that charming consideration which serves to distinguish the truly pious from the wolves that perish, exclaimed:

"If I could have my way, I'd blow up all your gods with dynamite."

"And if I could have mine," retorted the Heathen in His Blindness, bitterly malevolent but oleaginously suave, "I'd fan all yours out of the universe."

The Desperate Object

A Dishonest Gain was driving in its luxurious carriage through its private park, when it saw something which frantically and repeatedly ran against a stone wall, endeavouring to butt out its brains.

"Hold! Hold! thou desperate Object," cried the Dishonest Gain; "these beautiful private grounds are no place for such work as thine."

"True," said the Object, pausing; "I have other and better grounds for it."

"Then thou art a happy man," said the Dishonest Gain, "and thy bleeding head is but mere dissembling. Who art thou, great actor?"

"I am known," said the Object, dashing itself again at the wall, "as the Consciousness of Duty Well Performed."

The Appropriate Memorial

A High Public Functionary having died, the citizens of his town held a meeting to consider how to honour his memory, and an Other High Public Functionary rose and addressed the meeting.

"Mr. Chairman and Gintlemen," said the Other, "it sames to me, and I'm hopin' yez wull approve the suggestion, that an appropriet way to honour the mimory of the deceased would be to erect an emolument sootably inscribed wid his vartues."

The soul of the great man looked down from Heaven and wept.

A Needless Labour

After waiting many a weary day to revenge himself upon a Lion for some unconsidered manifestation of contempt, a Skunk finally saw him coming, and posting himself in the path ahead uttered the inaudible discord of his race. Observing that the Lion gave no attention to the matter, the Skunk, keeping carefully out of reach, said:

"Sir, I beg leave to point out that I have set on foot an implacable odour."

"My dear fellow," the Lion replied, "you have taken a needless trouble; I already knew that you were a Skunk."

A Flourishing Industry

"Are the industries of this country in a flourishing condition?" asked a Traveller from a Foreign Land of the first man he met in America.

"Splendid!" said the Man. "I have more orders than I can fill."

"What is your business?" the Traveller from a Foreign Land inquired.

The Man replied, "I make boxing-gloves for the tongues of pugilists."

The Self-Made Monkey

A Man of humble birth and no breeding, who held a high political office, was passing through a forest, when he met a Monkey.

"I take it you are one of my constituents," the Man said.

"No," replied the Monkey; "but I will support you if you urge a valid claim to my approval."

"I am a self-made man," said the other, proudly.

"That is nothing," the Monkey said. And going to a bigger pine, he rose by his own unaided exertions to the top branch, where he sat, all bedaubed with the pitch which that vegetable exudes. "Now," he added, "I am a self-made Monkey."

The Patriot and the Banker

A Patriot who had taken office poor and retired rich was introduced at a bank where he desired to open an account.

"With pleasure," said the Honest Banker; "we shall be glad to do business with you; but first you must make yourself an honest man by restoring what you stole from the Government."

"Good heavens!" cried the Patriot; "if I do that, I shall have nothing to deposit with you."

"I don't see that," the Honest Banker replied. "We are not the whole American people."

"Ah, I understand," said the Patriot, musing. "At what sum do you estimate this bank's proportion of the country's loss by me?"

"About a dollar," answered the Honest Banker.

And with a proud consciousness of serving his country wisely and well he charged that sum to the account.

The Mourning Brothers

Observing that he was about to die, an Old Man called his two Sons to his bedside and expounded the situation.

"My children," said he, "you have not shown me many marks of respect during my life, but you will attest your sorrow for my death. To him who the longer wears a weed upon his hat in memory of me shall go my entire fortune. I have made a will to that effect."

So when the Old Man was dead each of the youths put a weed upon his hat and wore it until he was himself old, when, seeing that neither would give in, they agreed that the younger should leave off his weeds and the elder give him half of the estate. But when the elder applied for the property he found that there had been an Executor!

Thus were hypocrisy and obstinacy fitly punished.

The Disinterested Arbiter

Two Dogs who had been fighting for a bone, without advantage to either, referred their dispute to a Sheep. The Sheep patiently heard their statements, then flung the bone into a pond.

"Why did you do that?" said the Dogs.

"Because," replied the Sheep, "I am a vegetarian."

The Thief and the Honest Man

A Thief who had brought a suit against his accomplices to recover his share of the plunder taken from an Honest Man, demanded the Honest Man's attendance at the trial to testify to his loss. But the Honest Man explained that as he was merely the agent of a company of other honest men it was none of his affair; and when the officers came to serve him with a subpœna he hid himself behind his back and wiled away the dragging hours of retirement and inaction by picking his own pockets.

The Dutiful Son

A Millionaire who had gone to an almshouse to visit his father met a Neighbour there, who was greatly surprised.

"What!" said the Neighbour, "you do sometimes visit your father?"

"If our situations were reversed," said the Millionaire, "I am sure he would visit me. The old man has always been rather proud of me. Besides," he added, softly, "I had to have his signature; I am insuring his life."

AESOPUS

EMENDATUS

The Cat and the Youth

A Cat fell in love with a handsome Young Man, and entreated Venus to change her into a woman.

"I should think," said Venus, "you might make so trifling a change without bothering me. However, be a woman."

Afterward, wishing to see if the change were complete, Venus caused a mouse to approach, whereupon the woman shrieked and made such a show of herself that the Young Man would not marry her.

The Farmer and His Sons

A Farmer being about to die, and knowing that during his illness his Sons had permitted the vineyard to become overgrown with weeds while they improved the shining hour by gambling with the doctor, said to them:

"My boys, there is a great treasure buried in the vineyard. You dig in the ground until you find it."

So the Sons dug up all the weeds, and all the vines too, and even neglected to bury the old man.

Jupiter and the Baby Show

Jupiter held a baby show, open to all animals, and a Monkey entered her hideous cub for a prize, but Jupiter only laughed at her.

"It is all very well," said the Monkey, "to laugh at my offspring, but you go into any gallery of antique sculpture and look at the statues and busts of the fellows that you begot yourself."

"'Sh! don't expose me," said Jupiter, and awarded her the first prize.

The Man and the Dog

A Man who had been bitten by a Dog was told that the wound would heal if he would dip a piece of bread in the blood and give it to the Dog. He did so.

"No," said the Dog; "if I were to accept that, it might be thought that in biting you I was actuated by improper motives."

"And by what motives were you actuated?" asked the Man.

"I desired," replied the Dog, "merely to harmonise myself with the Divine Scheme of Things. I'm a child of Nature."

The Cat and the Birds

Hearing that the Birds in an aviary were ill, a Cat went to them and said that he was a physician, and would cure them if they would let him in.

"To what school of medicine do you belong?" asked the Birds.

"I am a Miaulopathist," said the Cat.

"Did you ever practise Gohomœopathy?" the Birds inquired, winking faintly.

The Cat took the hint and his leave.

Mercury and the Woodchopper

A Woodchopper, who had dropped his axe into a deep pool, besought Mercury to recover it for him. That thoughtless deity immediately plunged into the pool, which became so salivated that the trees about its margin all came loose and dropped out.

The Fox and the Grapes

A fox, seeing some sour grapes hanging within an inch of his nose, and being unwilling to admit that there was anything he would not eat, solemnly declared that they were out of his reach.

The Penitent Thief

A Boy who had been taught by his Mother to steal grew to be a man and was a professional public official. One day he was taken in the act and condemned to die. While going to the place of execution he passed his Mother and said to her:

"Behold your work! If you had not taught me to steal, I should not have come to this."

"Indeed!" said the Mother. "And who, pray, taught you to be detected?"

The Archer and the Eagle

An Eagle mortally wounded by an Archer was greatly comforted to observe that the arrow was feathered with one of his own quills.

"I should have felt bad, indeed," he said, "to think that any other eagle had a hand in this."

Truth and the Traveller

A Man travelling in a desert met a Woman.

"Who art thou?" asked the Man, "and why dost thou dwell in this dreadful place?"

"My name," replied the Woman, "is Truth; and I live in the desert in order to be near my worshippers when they are driven from among their fellows. They all come, sooner or later."

"Well," said the Man, looking about, "the country doesn't seem to be very thickly settled here."

The Wolf and the Lamb

A Lamb, pursued by a Wolf, fled into the temple.

"The priest will catch you and sacrifice you," said the Wolf, "if you remain there."

"It is just as well to be sacrificed by the priest as to be eaten by you," said the Lamb.

"My friend," said the Wolf, "it pains me to see you considering so great a question from a purely selfish point of view. It is not just as well for me."

The Lion and the Boar

A Lion and a Boar, who were fighting for water at a pool, saw some vultures hovering significantly above them. "Let us make up our quarrel," said the Boar, "or these fellows will get one of us, sure."

"I should not so much mind that," replied the Lion, "if they would get the right one. However, I am willing to stop fighting, and then perhaps I can grab a vulture. I like chicken better than pork, anyhow."

The Grasshopper and the Ant

One day in winter a hungry Grasshopper applied to an Ant for some of the food which they had stored.

"Why," said the Ant, "did you not store up some food for yourself, instead of singing all the time?"

"So I did," said the Grasshopper; "so I did; but you fellows broke in and carried it all away."

The Fisher and the Fished

A Fisherman who had caught a very small Fish was putting it in his basket when it said:

"I pray you put me back into the stream, for I can be of no use to you; the gods do not eat fish."

"But I am no god," said the Fisherman.

"True," said the Fish, "but as soon as Jupiter has heard of your exploit, he will elevate you to the deitage. You are the only man that ever caught a small fish."

The Farmer and the Fox

A Farmer who had a deadly and implacable hatred against a certain Fox, caught him and tied some tow to his tail; then carrying him to the centre of his own grain-field, set the tow on fire and let the animal go.

"Alas!" said the Farmer, seeing the result; "if that grain had not been heavily insured, I might have had to dissemble my hatred of the Fox."

Dame Fortune and the Traveller

A weary Traveller who had lain down and fallen asleep on the brink of a deep well was discovered by Dame Fortune.

"If this fool," she said, "should have an uneasy dream and roll into the well men would say that I did it. It is painful to me to be unjustly accused, and I shall see that I am not."

So saying she rolled the man into the well.

The Victor and the Victim

Two Game Cocks, having fought a battle, the defeated one skulked away and hid, but the victor mounted a wall and crowed lustily. This attracted the attention of a hawk, who said:

"Behold! how pride goeth before a fall."

So he swooped down upon the boasting bird and was about to destroy him, when the vanquished Cock came out of his hiding place, and between the two the Hawk was calamitously defeated.

The Wolf and the Shepherds

A Wolf passing a Shepherd's hut looked in and saw the shepherds dining.

"Come in," said one of them, ironically, "and partake of your favourite dish, a haunch of mutton."

"Thank you," said the Wolf, moving away, "but you must excuse me; I have just had a saddle of shepherd."

The Goose and the Swan

A certain rich man reared a Goose and a Swan, the one for his table, the other because she was reputed a good singer. One night when the Cook went to kill the Goose he got hold of the Swan instead. Thereupon the Swan, to induce him to spare her life, began to sing; but she saved him nothing but the trouble of killing her, for she died of the song.

The Lion, the Cock, and the Ass

A Lion was about to attack a braying Ass, when a Cock near by crowed shrilly, and the Lion ran away. "What frightened him?" the Ass asked.

"Lions have a superstitious terror of my voice," answered the Cock, proudly.

"Well, well, well," said the Ass, shaking his head; "I should think that any animal that is afraid of your voice and doesn't mind mine must have an uncommon kind of ear."

The Snake and the Swallow

A Swallow who had built her nest in a court of justice reared a fine family of young birds. One day a Snake came out of a chink in the wall and was about to eat them. The Just Judge at once issued an injunction, and making an order for their removal to his own house, ate them himself.

The Wolves and the Dogs

"Why should there be strife between us?" said the Wolves to the Sheep. "It is all owing to those quarrelsome dogs. Dismiss them, and we shall have peace."

"You seem to think," replied the Sheep, "that it is an easy thing to dismiss dogs. Have you always found it so?"

The Hen and the Vipers

A Hen who had patiently hatched out a brood of vipers, was accosted by a Swallow, who said: "What a fool you are to give life to creatures who will reward you by destroying you."

"I am a little bit on the destroy myself," said the Hen, tranquilly swallowing one of the little reptiles; "and it is not an act of folly to provide oneself with the delicacies of the season."

A Seasonable Joke

A Spendthrift, seeing a single swallow, pawned his cloak, thinking that Summer was at hand. It was.

The Lion and the Thorn

A Lion roaming through the forest got a thorn in his foot, and, meeting a Shepherd, asked him to remove it. The Shepherd did so, and the Lion, having just surfeited himself on another shepherd, went away without harming him. Some time afterward the Shepherd was condemned on a false accusation to be cast to the lions in the amphitheatre. When they were about to devour him, one of them said:

"This is the man who removed the thorn from my foot."

Hearing this, the others honourably abstained, and the claimant ate the Shepherd all himself.

The Fawn and the Buck

A Fawn said to its father: "You are larger, stronger, and more active than a dog, and you have sharp horns. Why do you run away when you hear one barking?"

"Because, my child," replied the Buck, "my temper is so uncertain that if I permit one of those noisy creatures to come into my presence I am likely to forget myself and do him an injury."

The Kite, the Pigeons, and the Hawk

Some Pigeons exposed to the attacks of a Kite asked a Hawk to defend them. He consented, and being admitted into the cote waited for the Kite, whom he fell upon and devoured. When he was so surfeited that he could scarcely move, the grateful Pigeons scratched out his eyes.

The Wolf and the Babe

A Famishing Wolf, passing the door of a cottage in the forest, heard a Mother say to her babe:

"Be quiet, or I will throw you out of the window, and the wolves will get you."

So he waited all day below the window, growing more hungry all the time. But at night the Old Man, having returned from the village club, threw out both Mother and Child.

The Wolf and the Ostrich

A Wolf, who in devouring a man had choked himself with a bunch of keys, asked an ostrich to put her head down his throat and pull them out, which she did.

"I suppose," said the Wolf, "you expect payment for that service."

"A kind act," replied the Ostrich, "is its own reward; I have eaten the keys."

The Herdsman and the Lion

A Herdsman who had lost a bullock entreated the gods to bring him the thief, and vowed he would sacrifice a goat to them. Just then a Lion, his jaws dripping with bullock's blood, approached the Herdsman.

"I thank you, good deities," said the Herdsman, continuing his prayer, "for showing me the thief. And now if you will take him away, I will stand another goat."

The Man and the Viper

A Man finding a frozen Viper put it into his bosom.

"The coldness of the human heart," he said, with a grin, "will keep the creature in his present condition until I can reach home and revive him on the coals."

But the pleasures of hope so fired his heart that the Viper thawed, and sliding to the ground thanked the Man civilly for his hospitality and glided away.

The Man and the Eagle

An Eagle was once captured by a Man, who clipped his wings and put him in the poultry yard, along with the chickens. The Eagle was much depressed in spirits by the change.

"Why should you not rather rejoice?" said the Man. "You were only an ordinary fellow as an eagle; but as an old rooster you are a fowl of incomparable distinction."

The War-Horse and the Miller

Having heard that the State was about to be invaded by a hostile army, a War-horse belonging to a Colonel of the Militia offered his services to a passing Miller.

"No," said the patriotic Miller, "I will employ no one who deserts his position in the hour of danger. It is sweet to die for one's country."

Something in the sentiment sounded familiar, and, looking at the Miller more closely, the War-horse recognised his master in disguise.

The Dog and the Reflection

A Dog passing over a stream on a plank saw his reflection in the water.

"You ugly brute!" he cried; "how dare you look at me in that insolent way."

He made a grab in the water, and, getting hold of what he supposed was the other dog's lip, lifted out a fine piece of meat which a butcher's boy had dropped into the stream.

The Man and the Fish-Horn

A Truthful Man, finding a musical instrument in the road, asked the name of it, and was told that it was a fish-horn. The next time he went fishing he set his nets and blew the fish-horn all day to charm the fish into them; but at nightfall there were not only no fish in his nets, but none along that part of the coast. Meeting a friend while on his way home he was asked what luck he had had.

"Well," said the Truthful Man, "the weather is not right for fishing, but it's a red-letter day for music."

The Hare and the Tortoise

A Hare having ridiculed the slow movements of a Tortoise, was challenged by the latter to run a race, a Fox to go to the goal and be the judge. They got off well together, the hare at the top of her speed, the Tortoise, who had no other intention than making his antagonist exert herself, going very leisurely. After sauntering along for some time he discovered the Hare by the wayside, apparently asleep, and seeing a chance to win pushed on as fast as he could, arriving at the goal hours afterwards, suffering from extreme fatigue and claiming the victory.

"Not so," said the Fox; "the Hare was here long ago, and went back to cheer you on your way."

Hercules and the Carter

A Carter was driving a waggon loaded with a merchant's goods, when the wheels stuck in a rut. Thereupon he began to pray to Hercules, without other exertion.

"Indolent fellow!" said Hercules; "you ask me to help you, but will not help yourself."

So the Carter helped himself to so many of the most valuable goods that the horses easily ran away with the remainder.

The Lion and the Bull

A Lion wishing to lure a Bull to a place where it would be safe to attack him, said: "My friend, I have killed a fine sheep; will you come with me and partake of the mutton?"

"With pleasure," said the Bull, "as soon as you have refreshed yourself a little for the journey. Pray have some grass."

The Man and His Goose

"See these valuable golden eggs," said a Man that owned a Goose. "Surely a Goose which can lay such eggs as those must have a gold mine inside her."

So he killed the Goose and cut her open, but found that she was just like any other goose. Moreover, on examining the eggs that she had laid he found they were just like any other eggs.

The Wolf and the Feeding Goat

A Wolf saw a Goat feeding at the summit of a rock, where he could not get at her.

"Why do you stay up there in that sterile place and go hungry?" said the Wolf. "Down here where I am the broken-bottle vine cometh up as a flower, the celluloid collar blossoms as the rose, and the tin-can tree brings forth after its kind."

"That is true, no doubt," said the Goat, "but how about the circus-poster crop? I hear that it failed this year down there."

The Wolf, perceiving that he was being chaffed, went away and resumed his duties at the doors of the poor.

Jupiter and the Birds

Jupiter commanded all the birds to appear before him, so that he might choose the most beautiful to be their king. The ugly Jackdaw, collecting all the fine feathers which had fallen from the other birds, attached them to his own body and appeared at the examination, looking very gay. The other birds, recognising their own borrowed plumage, indignantly protested, and began to strip him.

"Hold!" said Jupiter; "this self-made bird has more sense than any of you. He is your king."

The Lion and the Mouse

A Lion who had caught a Mouse was about to kill him, when the Mouse said:

"If you will spare my life, I will do as much for you some day."

The Lion good-naturedly let him go. It happened shortly afterwards that the Lion was caught by some hunters and bound with cords. The Mouse, passing that way, and seeing that his benefactor was helpless, gnawed off his tail.

The Old Man and His Sons

An Old Man, afflicted with a family of contentious Sons, brought in a bundle of sticks and asked the young men to break it. After repeated efforts they confessed that it could not be done. "Behold," said the Old Man, "the advantage of unity; as long as these sticks are in alliance they are invincible, but observe how feeble they are individually."

Pulling a single stick from the bundle, he broke it easily upon the head of the eldest Son, and this he repeated until all had been served.

The Crab and His Son

A Logical Crab said to his Son, "Why do you not walk straight forward? Your sidelong gait is singularly ungraceful."

"Why don't you walk straight forward yourself," said the Son.

"Erring youth," replied the Logical Crab, "you are introducing new and irrelevant matter."

The North Wind and the Sun

The Sun and the North Wind disputed which was the more powerful, and agreed that he should be declared victor who could the sooner strip a traveller of his clothes. So they waited until a traveller came by. But the traveller had been indiscreet enough to stay over night at a summer hotel, and had no clothes.

The Mountain and the Mouse

A Mountain was in labour, and the people of seven cities had assembled to watch its movements and hear its groans. While they waited in breathless expectancy out came a Mouse.

"Oh, what a baby!" they cried in derision.

"I may be a baby," said the Mouse, gravely, as he passed outward through the forest of shins, "but I know tolerably well how to diagnose a volcano."

The Bellamy and the Members

The Members of a body of Socialists rose in insurrection against their Bellamy.

"Why," said they, "should we be all the time tucking you out with food when you do nothing to tuck us out?"

So, resolving to take no further action, they went away, and looking backward had the satisfaction to see the Bellamy compelled to sell his own book.

OLD SAWS

WITH NEW TEETH

The Wolf and the Crane

A Rich Man wanted to tell a certain lie, but the lie was of such monstrous size that it stuck in his throat; so he employed an Editor to write it out and publish it in his paper as an editorial. But when the Editor presented his bill, the Rich Man said:

"Be content—is it nothing that I refrained from advising you about investments?"

The Lion and the Mouse

A Judge was awakened by the noise of a lawyer prosecuting a Thief. Rising in wrath he was about to sentence the Thief to life imprisonment when the latter said:

"I beg that you will set me free, and I will some day requite your kindness."

Pleased and flattered to be bribed, although by nothing but an empty promise, the Judge let him go. Soon afterward he found that it was more than an empty promise, for, having become a Thief, he was himself set free by the other, who had become a Judge.

The Hares and the Frogs

The Members of a Legislature, being told that they were the meanest thieves in the world, resolved to commit suicide. So they bought shrouds, and laying them in a convenient place prepared to cut their throats. While they were grinding their razors some Tramps passing that way stole the shrouds.

"Let us live, my friends," said one of the Legislators to the others; "the world is better than we thought. It contains meaner thieves than we."

The Belly and the Members

Some Workingmen employed in a shoe factory went on a strike, saying: "Why should we continue to work to feed and clothe our employer when we have none too much to eat and wear ourselves?"

The Manufacturer, seeing that he could get no labour for a long time and finding the times pretty hard anyhow, burned down his shoe factory for the insurance, and when the strikers wanted to resume work there was no work to resume. So they boycotted a tanner.

The Piping Fisherman

An Editor who was always vaunting the purity, enterprise, and fearlessness of his paper was pained to observe that he got no subscribers. One day it occurred to him to stop saying that his paper was pure and enterprising and fearless, and make it so. "If these are not good qualities," he reasoned, "it is folly to claim them."

Under the new policy he got so many subscribers that his rivals endeavoured to discover the secret of his prosperity, but he kept it, and when he died it died with him.

The Ants and the Grasshopper

Some Members of a Legislature were making schedules of their wealth at the end of the session, when an Honest Miner came along and asked them to divide with him. The members of the Legislature inquired:

"Why did you not acquire property of your own?"

"Because," replied the Honest Miner, "I was so busy digging out gold that I had no leisure to lay up something worth while."

Then the Members of the Legislature derided him, saying: "If you waste your time in profitless amusement, you cannot, of course, expect to share the rewards of industry."

The Dog and His Reflection

A State Official carrying off the Dome of the Capitol met the Ghost of his predecessor, who had come out of his political grave to warn him that God saw him. As the place of meeting was lonely and the time midnight, the State Official set down the Dome of the Capitol, and commanded the supposed traveller to throw up his hands. The Ghost replied that he had not eaten them, and while he was explaining the situation another State Official silently added the dome to his own collection.

The Lion, the Bear, and the Fox

Two Thieves having stolen a Piano and being unable to divide it fairly without a remainder went to law about it and continued the contest as long as either one could steal a dollar to bribe the judge. When they could give no more an Honest Man came along and by a single small payment obtained a judgment and took the Piano home, where his daughter used it to develop her biceps muscles, becoming a famous pugiliste.

The Ass and the Lion's Skin

A member of the State Militia stood at a street corner, scowling stormily, and the people passing that way went a long way around him, thinking of the horrors of war. But presently, in order to terrify them still more, he strode toward them, when, his sword entangling his legs, he fell upon the field of glory, and the people passed over him singing their sweetest songs.

The Ass and the Grasshoppers

A Statesman heard some Labourers singing at their work, and wishing to be happy too, asked them what made them so.

"Honesty," replied the Labourers.

So the Statesman resolved that he too would be honest, and the result was that he died of want.

The Wolf and the Lion

An Indian who had been driven out of a fertile valley by a White Settler, said:

"Now that you have robbed me of my land, there is nothing for me to do but issue invitations to a war-dance."

"I don't so much mind your dancing," said the White Settler, putting a fresh cartridge into his rifle, "but if you attempt to make me dance you will become a good Indian lamented by all who didn't know you. How did *you* get this land, anyhow?"

The Indian's claim was compromised for a plug hat and a tin horn.

The Hare and the Tortoise

Of two Writers one was brilliant but indolent; the other, though dull, industrious. They set out for the goal of fame with equal opportunities. Before they died the brilliant one was detected in seventy languages as the author of but two or three books of fiction and poetry, while the other was honoured in the Bureau of Statistics of his native land as the compiler of sixteen volumes of tabulated information relating to the domestic hog.

The Milkmaid and Her Bucket

A Senator fell to musing as follows: "With the money which I shall get for my vote in favour of the bill to subsidise cat-ranches, I can buy a kit of burglar's tools and open a bank. The profit of that enterprise will enable me to obtain a long, low, black schooner, raise a death's-head flag and engage in commerce on the high seas. From my gains in that business I can pay for the Presidency, which at $50,000 a year will give me in four years—" but it took him so long to make the calculation that the bill to subsidise cat-ranches passed without his vote, and he was compelled to return to his constituents an honest man, tormented with a clean conscience.

King Log and King Stork

The People being dissatisfied with a Democratic Legislature, which stole no more than they had, elected a Republican one, which not only stole all they had but exacted a promissory note for the balance due, secured by a mortgage upon their hope of death.

The Wolf Who Would Be a Lion

A Foolish Fellow who had been told that he was a great man believed it, and got himself appointed a Commissioner to the Interasylum Exposition of Preserved Idiots. At the first meeting of the Board he was mistaken for one of the exhibits, and the janitor was ordered to remove him to his appropriate glass case.

"Alas!" he exclaimed as he was carried out, "why was I not content to remain where the cut of my forehead is so common as to be known as the Pacific Slope?"

The Monkey and the Nuts

A certain City desiring to purchase a site for a public Deformatory procured an appropriation from the Government of the country. Deeming this insufficient for purchase of the site and payment of reasonable commissions to themselves, the men in charge of the matter asked for a larger sum, which was readily given. Believing that the fountain could not be dipped dry, they applied for still more and more yet. Wearied at last by their importunities, the Government said it would be damned if it gave anything. So it gave nothing and was damned all the harder.

The Boys and the Frogs

Some editors of newspapers were engaged in diffusing general intelligence and elevating the moral sentiment of the public. They had been doing this for some time, when an Eminent Statesman stuck his head out of the pool of politics, and, speaking for the members of his profession, said:

"My friends, I beg you will desist. I know you make a great deal of money by this kind of thing, but consider the damage you inflict upon the business of others!"

A CATALOGUE OF SELECTED DOVER BOOKS
IN ALL FIELDS OF INTEREST

A CATALOGUE OF SELECTED DOVER BOOKS
IN ALL FIELDS OF INTEREST

AMERICA'S OLD MASTERS, James T. Flexner. Four men emerged unexpectedly from provincial 18th century America to leadership in European art: Benjamin West, J. S. Copley, C. R. Peale, Gilbert Stuart. Brilliant coverage of lives and contributions. Revised, 1967 edition. 69 plates. 365pp. of text.

21806-6 Paperbound $2.75

FIRST FLOWERS OF OUR WILDERNESS: AMERICAN PAINTING, THE COLONIAL PERIOD, James T. Flexner. Painters, and regional painting traditions from earliest Colonial times up to the emergence of Copley, West and Peale Sr., Foster, Gustavus Hesselius, Feke, John Smibert and many anonymous painters in the primitive manner. Engaging presentation, with 162 illustrations. xxii + 368pp.

22180-6 Paperbound $3.50

THE LIGHT OF DISTANT SKIES: AMERICAN PAINTING, 1760-1835, James T. Flexner. The great generation of early American painters goes to Europe to learn and to teach: West, Copley, Gilbert Stuart and others. Allston, Trumbull, Morse; also contemporary American painters—primitives, derivatives, academics—who remained in America. 102 illustrations. xiii + 306pp.

22179-2 Paperbound $3.00

A HISTORY OF THE RISE AND PROGRESS OF THE ARTS OF DESIGN IN THE UNITED STATES, William Dunlap. Much the richest mine of information on early American painters, sculptors, architects, engravers, miniaturists, etc. The only source of information for scores of artists, the major primary source for many others. Unabridged reprint of rare original 1834 edition, with new introduction by James T. Flexner, and 394 new illustrations. Edited by Rita Weiss. 6⅝ x 9⅝.

21695-0, 21696-9, 21697-7 Three volumes, Paperbound $13.50

EPOCHS OF CHINESE AND JAPANESE ART, Ernest F. Fenollosa. From primitive Chinese art to the 20th century, thorough history, explanation of every important art period and form, including Japanese woodcuts; main stress on China and Japan, but Tibet, Korea also included. Still unexcelled for its detailed, rich coverage of cultural background, aesthetic elements, diffusion studies, particularly of the historical period. 2nd, 1913 edition. 242 illustrations. lii + 439pp. of text.

20364-6, 20365-4 Two volumes, Paperbound $5.00

THE GENTLE ART OF MAKING ENEMIES, James A. M. Whistler. Greatest wit of his day deflates Oscar Wilde, Ruskin, Swinburne; strikes back at inane critics, exhibitions, art journalism; aesthetics of impressionist revolution in most striking form. Highly readable classic by great painter. Reproduction of edition designed by Whistler. Introduction by Alfred Werner. xxxvi + 334pp.

21875-9 Paperbound $2.25

VISUAL ILLUSIONS: THEIR CAUSES, CHARACTERISTICS, AND APPLICATIONS, Matthew Luckiesh. Thorough description and discussion of optical illusion, geometric and perspective, particularly; size and shape distortions, illusions of color, of motion; natural illusions; use of illusion in art and magic, industry, etc. Most useful today with op art, also for classical art. Scores of effects illustrated. Introduction by William H. Ittleson. 100 illustrations. xxi + 252pp.

21530-X Paperbound $1.50

A HANDBOOK OF ANATOMY FOR ART STUDENTS, Arthur Thomson. Thorough, virtually exhaustive coverage of skeletal structure, musculature, etc. Full text, supplemented by anatomical diagrams and drawings and by photographs of undraped figures. Unique in its comparison of male and female forms, pointing out differences of contour, texture, form. 211 figures, 40 drawings, 86 photographs. xx + 459pp. 5⅜ x 8⅜.

21163-0 Paperbound $3.00

150 MASTERPIECES OF DRAWING, Selected by Anthony Toney. Full page reproductions of drawings from the early 16th to the end of the 18th century, all beautifully reproduced: Rembrandt, Michelangelo, Dürer, Fragonard, Urs, Graf, Wouwerman, many others. First-rate browsing book, model book for artists. xviii + 150pp. 8⅜ x 11¼.

21032-4 Paperbound $2.00

THE LATER WORK OF AUBREY BEARDSLEY, Aubrey Beardsley. Exotic, erotic, ironic masterpieces in full maturity: Comedy Ballet, Venus and Tannhauser, Pierrot, Lysistrata, Rape of the Lock, Savoy material, Ali Baba, Volpone, etc. This material revolutionized the art world, and is still powerful, fresh, brilliant. With *The Early Work*, all Beardsley's finest work. 174 plates, 2 in color. xiv + 176pp. 8⅛ x 11.

21817-1 Paperbound $3.00

DRAWINGS OF REMBRANDT, Rembrandt van Rijn. Complete reproduction of fabulously rare edition by Lippmann and Hofstede de Groot, completely reedited, updated, improved by Prof. Seymour Slive, Fogg Museum. Portraits, Biblical sketches, landscapes, Oriental types, nudes, episodes from classical mythology—All Rembrandt's fertile genius. Also selection of drawings by his pupils and followers. "Stunning volumes," *Saturday Review*. 550 illustrations. lxxviii + 552pp. 9⅛ x 12¼.

21485-0, 21486-9 Two volumes, Paperbound $6.50

THE DISASTERS OF WAR, Francisco Goya. One of the masterpieces of Western civilization—83 etchings that record Goya's shattering, bitter reaction to the Napoleonic war that swept through Spain after the insurrection of 1808 and to war in general. Reprint of the first edition, with three additional plates from Boston's Museum of Fine Arts. All plates facsimile size. Introduction by Philip Hofer, Fogg Museum. v + 97pp. 9⅜ x 8¼.

21872-4 Paperbound $1.75

GRAPHIC WORKS OF ODILON REDON. Largest collection of Redon's graphic works ever assembled: 172 lithographs, 28 etchings and engravings, 9 drawings. These include some of his most famous works. All the plates from *Odilon Redon: oeuvre graphique complet,* plus additional plates. New introduction and caption translations by Alfred Werner. 209 illustrations. xxvii + 209pp. 9⅛ x 12¼.

21966-8 Paperbound $4.00

DESIGN BY ACCIDENT; A BOOK OF "ACCIDENTAL EFFECTS" FOR ARTISTS AND DESIGNERS, James F. O'Brien. Create your own unique, striking, imaginative effects by "controlled accident" interaction of materials: paints and lacquers, oil and water based paints, splatter, crackling materials, shatter, similar items. Everything you do will be different; first book on this limitless art, so useful to both fine artist and commercial artist. Full instructions. 192 plates showing "accidents," 8 in color. viii + 215pp. 8⅜ x 11¼. 21942-9 Paperbound $3.50

THE BOOK OF SIGNS, Rudolf Koch. Famed German type designer draws 493 beautiful symbols: religious, mystical, alchemical, imperial, property marks, runes, etc. Remarkable fusion of traditional and modern. Good for suggestions of timelessness, smartness, modernity. Text. vi + 104pp. 6⅛ x 9¼. 20162-7 Paperbound $1.25

HISTORY OF INDIAN AND INDONESIAN ART, Ananda K. Coomaraswamy. An unabridged republication of one of the finest books by a great scholar in Eastern art. Rich in descriptive material, history, social backgrounds; Sunga reliefs, Rajput paintings, Gupta temples, Burmese frescoes, textiles, jewelry, sculpture, etc. 400 photos. viii + 423pp. 6⅜ x 9¾. 21436-2 Paperbound $3.50

PRIMITIVE ART, Franz Boas. America's foremost anthropologist surveys textiles, ceramics, woodcarving, basketry, metalwork, etc.; patterns, technology, creation of symbols, style origins. All areas of world, but very full on Northwest Coast Indians. More than 350 illustrations of baskets, boxes, totem poles, weapons, etc. 378 pp. 20025-6 Paperbound $2.50

THE GENTLEMAN AND CABINET MAKER'S DIRECTOR, Thomas Chippendale. Full reprint (third edition, 1762) of most influential furniture book of all time, by master cabinetmaker. 200 plates, illustrating chairs, sofas, mirrors, tables, cabinets, plus 24 photographs of surviving pieces. Biographical introduction by N. Bienenstock. vi + 249pp. 9⅞ x 12¾. 21601-2 Paperbound $3.50

AMERICAN ANTIQUE FURNITURE, Edgar G. Miller, Jr. The basic coverage of all American furniture before 1840. Individual chapters cover type of furniture—clocks, tables, sideboards, etc.—chronologically, with inexhaustible wealth of data. More than 2100 photographs, all identified, commented on. Essential to all early American collectors. Introduction by H. E. Keyes. vi + 1106pp. 7⅞ x 10¾. 21599-7, 21600-4 Two volumes, Paperbound $7.50

PENNSYLVANIA DUTCH AMERICAN FOLK ART, Henry J. Kauffman. 279 photos, 28 drawings of tulipware, Fraktur script, painted tinware, toys, flowered furniture, quilts, samplers, hex signs, house interiors, etc. Full descriptive text. Excellent for tourist, rewarding for designer, collector. Map. 146pp. 7⅞ x 10¾. 21205-X Paperbound $2.00

EARLY NEW ENGLAND GRAVESTONE RUBBINGS, Edmund V. Gillon, Jr. 43 photographs, 226 carefully reproduced rubbings show heavily symbolic, sometimes macabre early gravestones, up to early 19th century. Remarkable early American primitive art, occasionally strikingly beautiful; always powerful. Text. xxvi + 207pp. 8⅜ x 11¼. 21380-3 Paperbound $3.00

ALPHABETS AND ORNAMENTS, Ernst Lehner. Well-known pictorial source for decorative alphabets, script examples, cartouches, frames, decorative title pages, calligraphic initials, borders, similar material. 14th to 19th century, mostly European. Useful in almost any graphic arts designing, varied styles. 750 illustrations. 256pp. 7 x 10. 21905-4 Paperbound $3.50

PAINTING: A CREATIVE APPROACH, Norman Colquhoun. For the beginner simple guide provides an instructive approach to painting: major stumbling blocks for beginner; overcoming them, technical points; paints and pigments; oil painting; watercolor and other media and color. New section on "plastic" paints. Glossary. Formerly *Paint Your Own Pictures*. 221pp. 22000-1 Paperbound $1.75

THE ENJOYMENT AND USE OF COLOR, Walter Sargent. Explanation of the relations between colors themselves and between colors in nature and art, including hundreds of little-known facts about color values, intensities, effects of high and low illumination, complementary colors. Many practical hints for painters, references to great masters. 7 color plates, 29 illustrations. x + 274pp. 20944-X Paperbound $2.50

THE NOTEBOOKS OF LEONARDO DA VINCI, compiled and edited by Jean Paul Richter. 1566 extracts from original manuscripts reveal the full range of Leonardo's versatile genius: all his writings on painting, sculpture, architecture, anatomy, astronomy, geography, topography, physiology, mining, music, etc., in both Italian and English, with 186 plates of manuscript pages and more than 500 additional drawings. Includes studies for the Last Supper, the lost Sforza monument, and other works. Total of xlvii + 866pp. 7⅞ x 10¾. 22572-0, 22573-9 Two volumes, Paperbound $10.00

MONTGOMERY WARD CATALOGUE OF 1895. Tea gowns, yards of flannel and pillow-case lace, stereoscopes, books of gospel hymns, the New Improved Singer Sewing Machine, side saddles, milk skimmers, straight-edged razors, high-button shoes, spittoons, and on and on . . . listing some 25,000 items, practically all illustrated. Essential to the shoppers of the 1890's, it is our truest record of the spirit of the period. Unaltered reprint of Issue No. 57, Spring and Summer 1895. Introduction by Boris Emmet. Innumerable illustrations. xiii + 624pp. 8½ x 11⅝. 22377-9 Paperbound $6.95

THE CRYSTAL PALACE EXHIBITION ILLUSTRATED CATALOGUE (LONDON, 1851). One of the wonders of the modern world—the Crystal Palace Exhibition in which all the nations of the civilized world exhibited their achievements in the arts and sciences—presented in an equally important illustrated catalogue. More than 1700 items pictured with accompanying text—ceramics, textiles, cast-iron work, carpets, pianos, sleds, razors, wall-papers, billiard tables, beehives, silverware and hundreds of other artifacts—represent the focal point of Victorian culture in the Western World. Probably the largest collection of Victorian decorative art ever assembled—indispensable for antiquarians and designers. Unabridged republication of the Art-Journal Catalogue of the Great Exhibition of 1851, with all terminal essays. New introduction by John Gloag, F.S.A. xxxiv + 426pp. 9 x 12. 22503-8 Paperbound $4.50

A HISTORY OF COSTUME, Carl Köhler. Definitive history, based on surviving pieces of clothing primarily, and paintings, statues, etc. secondarily. Highly readable text, supplemented by 594 illustrations of costumes of the ancient Mediterranean peoples, Greece and Rome, the Teutonic prehistoric period; costumes of the Middle Ages, Renaissance, Baroque, 18th and 19th centuries. Clear, measured patterns are provided for many clothing articles. Approach is practical throughout. Enlarged by Emma von Sichart. 464pp. 21030-8 Paperbound $3.00

ORIENTAL RUGS, ANTIQUE AND MODERN, Walter A. Hawley. A complete and authoritative treatise on the Oriental rug—where they are made, by whom and how, designs and symbols, characteristics in detail of the six major groups, how to distinguish them and how to buy them. Detailed technical data is provided on periods, weaves, warps, wefts, textures, sides, ends and knots, although no technical background is required for an understanding. 11 color plates, 80 halftones, 4 maps. vi + 320pp. 6⅛ x 9⅛. 22366-3 Paperbound $5.00

TEN BOOKS ON ARCHITECTURE, Vitruvius. By any standards the most important book on architecture ever written. Early Roman discussion of aesthetics of building, construction methods, orders, sites, and every other aspect of architecture has inspired, instructed architecture for about 2,000 years. Stands behind Palladio, Michelangelo, Bramante, Wren, countless others. Definitive Morris H. Morgan translation. 68 illustrations. xii + 331pp. 20645-9 Paperbound $2.50

THE FOUR BOOKS OF ARCHITECTURE, Andrea Palladio. Translated into every major Western European language in the two centuries following its publication in 1570, this has been one of the most influential books in the history of architecture. Complete reprint of the 1738 Isaac Ware edition. New introduction by Adolf Placzek, Columbia Univ. 216 plates. xxii + 110pp. of text. 9½ x 12¾. 21308-0 Clothbound $10.00

STICKS AND STONES: A STUDY OF AMERICAN ARCHITECTURE AND CIVILIZATION, Lewis Mumford.One of the great classics of American cultural history. American architecture from the medieval-inspired earliest forms to the early 20th century; evolution of structure and style, and reciprocal influences on environment. 21 photographic illustrations. 238pp. 20202-X Paperbound $2.00

THE AMERICAN BUILDER'S COMPANION, Asher Benjamin. The most widely used early 19th century architectural style and source book, for colonial up into Greek Revival periods. Extensive development of geometry of carpentering, construction of sashes, frames, doors, stairs; plans and elevations of domestic and other buildings. Hundreds of thousands of houses were built according to this book, now invaluable to historians, architects, restorers, etc. 1827 edition. 59 plates. 114pp. 7⅞ x 10¾. 22236-5 Paperbound $3.00

DUTCH HOUSES IN THE HUDSON VALLEY BEFORE 1776, Helen Wilkinson Reynolds. The standard survey of the Dutch colonial house and outbuildings, with constructional features, decoration, and local history associated with individual homesteads. Introduction by Franklin D. Roosevelt. Map. 150 illustrations. 469pp. 6⅝ x 9¼. 21469-9 Paperbound $3.50

THE ARCHITECTURE OF COUNTRY HOUSES, Andrew J. Downing. Together with Vaux's *Villas and Cottages* this is the basic book for Hudson River Gothic architecture of the middle Victorian period. Full, sound discussions of general aspects of housing, architecture, style, decoration, furnishing, together with scores of detailed house plans, illustrations of specific buildings, accompanied by full text. Perhaps the most influential single American architectural book. 1850 edition. Introduction by J. Stewart Johnson. 321 figures, 34 architectural designs. xvi + 560pp.
22003-6 Paperbound $3.50

LOST EXAMPLES OF COLONIAL ARCHITECTURE, John Mead Howells. Full-page photographs of buildings that have disappeared or been so altered as to be denatured, including many designed by major early American architects. 245 plates. xvii + 248pp. 7⅞ x 10¾.
21143-6 Paperbound $3.00

DOMESTIC ARCHITECTURE OF THE AMERICAN COLONIES AND OF THE EARLY REPUBLIC, Fiske Kimball. Foremost architect and restorer of Williamsburg and Monticello covers nearly 200 homes between 1620-1825. Architectural details, construction, style features, special fixtures, floor plans, etc. Generally considered finest work in its area. 219 illustrations of houses, doorways, windows, capital mantels. xx + 314pp. 7⅞ x 10¾.
21743-4 Paperbound $3.50

EARLY AMERICAN ROOMS: 1650-1858, edited by Russell Hawes Kettell. Tour of 12 rooms, each representative of a different era in American history and each furnished, decorated, designed and occupied in the style of the era. 72 plans and elevations, 8-page color section, etc., show fabrics, wall papers, arrangements, etc. Full descriptive text. xvii + 200pp. of text. 8⅜ x 11¼.
21633-0 Paperbound $4.00

THE FITZWILLIAM VIRGINAL BOOK, edited by J. Fuller Maitland and W. B. Squire. Full modern printing of famous early 17th-century ms. volume of 300 works by Morley, Byrd, Bull, Gibbons, etc. For piano or other modern keyboard instrument; easy to read format. xxxvi + 938pp. 8⅜ x 11.
21068-5, 21069-3 Two volumes, Paperbound $8.00

HARPSICHORD MUSIC, Johann Sebastian Bach. Bach Gesellschaft edition. A rich selection of Bach's masterpieces for the harpsichord: the six English Suites, six French Suites, the six Partitas (Clavierübung part I), the Goldberg Variations (Clavierübung part IV), the fifteen Two-Part Inventions and the fifteen Three-Part Sinfonias. Clearly reproduced on large sheets with ample margins; eminently playable. vi + 312pp. 8⅛ x 11.
22360-4 Paperbound $5.00

THE MUSIC OF BACH: AN INTRODUCTION, Charles Sanford Terry. A fine, nontechnical introduction to Bach's music, both instrumental and vocal. Covers organ music, chamber music, passion music, other types. Analyzes themes, developments, innovations. x + 114pp.
21075-8 Paperbound $1.25

BEETHOVEN AND HIS NINE SYMPHONIES, Sir George Grove. Noted British musicologist provides best history, analysis, commentary on symphonies. Very thorough, rigorously accurate; necessary to both advanced student and amateur music lover. 436 musical passages. vii + 407 pp.
20334-4 Paperbound $2.25

JOHANN SEBASTIAN BACH, Philipp Spitta. One of the great classics of musicology, this definitive analysis of Bach's music (and life) has never been surpassed. Lucid, nontechnical analyses of hundreds of pieces (30 pages devoted to St. Matthew Passion, 26 to B Minor Mass). Also includes major analysis of 18th-century music. 450 musical examples. 40-page musical supplement. Total of xx + 1799pp.
(EUK) 22278-0, 22279-9 Two volumes, Clothbound $15.00

MOZART AND HIS PIANO CONCERTOS, Cuthbert Girdlestone. The only full-length study of an important area of Mozart's creativity. Provides detailed analyses of all 23 concertos, traces inspirational sources. 417 musical examples. Second edition. 509pp. (USO) 21271-8 Paperbound $3.50

THE PERFECT WAGNERITE: A COMMENTARY ON THE NIBLUNG'S RING, George Bernard Shaw. Brilliant and still relevant criticism in remarkable essays on Wagner's Ring cycle, Shaw's ideas on political and social ideology behind the plots, role of Leitmotifs, vocal requisites, etc. Prefaces. xxi + 136pp.
21707-8 Paperbound $1.50

DON GIOVANNI, W. A. Mozart. Complete libretto, modern English translation; biographies of composer and librettist; accounts of early performances and critical reaction. Lavishly illustrated. All the material you need to understand and appreciate this great work. Dover Opera Guide and Libretto Series; translated and introduced by Ellen Bleiler. 92 illustrations. 209pp.
21134-7 Paperbound $1.50

HIGH FIDELITY SYSTEMS: A LAYMAN'S GUIDE, Roy F. Allison. All the basic information you need for setting up your own audio system: high fidelity and stereo record players, tape records, F.M. Connections, adjusting tone arm, cartridge, checking needle alignment, positioning speakers, phasing speakers, adjusting hums, trouble-shooting, maintenance, and similar topics. Enlarged 1965 edition. More than 50 charts, diagrams, photos. iv + 91pp. 21514-8 Paperbound $1.25

REPRODUCTION OF SOUND, Edgar Villchur. Thorough coverage for laymen of high fidelity systems, reproducing systems in general, needles, amplifiers, preamps, loudspeakers, feedback, explaining physical background. "A rare talent for making technicalities vividly comprehensible," R. Darrell, *High Fidelity.* 69 figures. iv + 92pp. 21515-6 Paperbound $1.00

HEAR ME TALKIN' TO YA: THE STORY OF JAZZ AS TOLD BY THE MEN WHO MADE IT, Nat Shapiro and Nat Hentoff. Louis Armstrong, Fats Waller, Jo Jones, Clarence Williams, Billy Holiday, Duke Ellington, Jelly Roll Morton and dozens of other jazz greats tell how it was in Chicago's South Side, New Orleans, depression Harlem and the modern West Coast as jazz was born and grew. xvi + 429pp.
21726-4 Paperbound $2.00

FABLES OF AESOP, translated by Sir Roger L'Estrange. A reproduction of the very rare 1931 Paris edition; a selection of the most interesting fables, together with 50 imaginative drawings by Alexander Calder. v + 128pp. 6½x9¼.
21780-9 Paperbound $1.25

AGAINST THE GRAIN (A REBOURS), Joris K. Huysmans. Filled with weird images, evidences of a bizarre imagination, exotic experiments with hallucinatory drugs, rich tastes and smells and the diversions of its sybarite hero Duc Jean des Esseintes, this classic novel pushed 19th-century literary decadence to its limits. Full unabridged edition. Do not confuse this with abridged editions generally sold. Introduction by Havelock Ellis. xlix + 206pp.   22190-3 Paperbound $2.00

VARIORUM SHAKESPEARE: HAMLET. Edited by Horace H. Furness; a landmark of American scholarship. Exhaustive footnotes and appendices treat all doubtful words and phrases, as well as suggested critical emendations throughout the play's history. First volume contains editor's own text, collated with all Quartos and Folios. Second volume contains full first Quarto, translations of Shakespeare's sources (Belleforest, and Saxo Grammaticus), Der Bestrafte Brudermord, and many essays on critical and historical points of interest by major authorities of past and present. Includes details of staging and costuming over the years. By far the best edition available for serious students of Shakespeare. Total of xx + 905pp.
21004-9, 21005-7, 2 volumes, Paperbound $5.25

A LIFE OF WILLIAM SHAKESPEARE, Sir Sidney Lee. This is the standard life of Shakespeare, summarizing everything known about Shakespeare and his plays. Incredibly rich in material, broad in coverage, clear and judicious, it has served thousands as the best introduction to Shakespeare. 1931 edition. 9 plates. xxix + 792pp.   (USO) 21967-4 Paperbound $3.75

MASTERS OF THE DRAMA, John Gassner. Most comprehensive history of the drama in print, covering every tradition from Greeks to modern Europe and America, including India, Far East, etc. Covers more than 800 dramatists, 2000 plays, with biographical material, plot summaries, theatre history, criticism, etc. "Best of its kind in English," New Republic. 77 illustrations. xxii + 890pp.
20100-7 Clothbound $7.50

THE EVOLUTION OF THE ENGLISH LANGUAGE, George McKnight. The growth of English, from the 14th century to the present. Unusual, non-technical account presents basic information in very interesting form: sound shifts, change in grammar and syntax, vocabulary growth, similar topics. Abundantly illustrated with quotations. Formerly Modern English in the Making. xii + 590pp.
21932-1 Paperbound $3.50

AN ETYMOLOGICAL DICTIONARY OF MODERN ENGLISH, Ernest Weekley. Fullest, richest work of its sort, by foremost British lexicographer. Detailed word histories, including many colloquial and archaic words; extensive quotations. Do not confuse this with the Concise Etymological Dictionary, which is much abridged. Total of xxvii + 830pp. 6½ x 9¼.
21873-2, 21874-0 Two volumes, Paperbound $5.50

FLATLAND: A ROMANCE OF MANY DIMENSIONS, E. A. Abbott. Classic of science-fiction explores ramifications of life in a two-dimensional world, and what happens when a three-dimensional being intrudes. Amusing reading, but also useful as introduction to thought about hyperspace. Introduction by Banesh Hoffmann. 16 illustrations. xx + 103pp.   20001-9 Paperbound $1.00

POEMS OF ANNE BRADSTREET, edited with an introduction by Robert Hutchinson. A new selection of poems by America's first poet and perhaps the first significant woman poet in the English language. 48 poems display her development in works of considerable variety—love poems, domestic poems, religious meditations, formal elegies, "quaternions," etc. Notes, bibliography. viii + 222pp.

22160-1 Paperbound $2.00

THREE GOTHIC NOVELS: THE CASTLE OF OTRANTO BY HORACE WALPOLE; VATHEK BY WILLIAM BECKFORD; THE VAMPYRE BY JOHN POLIDORI, WITH FRAGMENT OF A NOVEL BY LORD BYRON, edited by E. F. Bleiler. The first Gothic novel, by Walpole; the finest Oriental tale in English, by Beckford; powerful Romantic supernatural story in versions by Polidori and Byron. All extremely important in history of literature; all still exciting, packed with supernatural thrills, ghosts, haunted castles, magic, etc. xl + 291pp.

21232-7 Paperbound $2.00

THE BEST TALES OF HOFFMANN, E. T. A. Hoffmann. 10 of Hoffmann's most important stories, in modern re-editings of standard translations: Nutcracker and the King of Mice, Signor Formica, Automata, The Sandman, Rath Krespel, The Golden Flowerpot, Master Martin the Cooper, The Mines of Falun, The King's Betrothed, A New Year's Eve Adventure. 7 illustrations by Hoffmann. Edited by E. F. Bleiler. xxxix + 419pp.

21793-0 Paperbound $2.25

GHOST AND HORROR STORIES OF AMBROSE BIERCE, Ambrose Bierce. 23 strikingly modern stories of the horrors latent in the human mind: The Eyes of the Panther, The Damned Thing, An Occurrence at Owl Creek Bridge, An Inhabitant of Carcosa, etc., plus the dream-essay, Visions of the Night. Edited by E. F. Bleiler. xxii + 199pp.

20767-6 Paperbound $1.50

BEST GHOST STORIES OF J. S. LEFANU, J. Sheridan LeFanu. Finest stories by Victorian master often considered greatest supernatural writer of all. Carmilla, Green Tea, The Haunted Baronet, The Familiar, and 12 others. Most never before available in the U. S. A. Edited by E. F. Bleiler. 8 illustrations from Victorian publications. xvii + 467pp.

20415-4 Paperbound $2.50

THE TIME STREAM, THE GREATEST ADVENTURE, AND THE PURPLE SAPPHIRE— THREE SCIENCE FICTION NOVELS, John Taine (Eric Temple Bell). Great American mathematician was also foremost science fiction novelist of the 1920's. *The Time Stream,* one of all-time classics, uses concepts of circular time; *The Greatest Adventure,* incredibly ancient biological experiments from Antarctica threaten to escape; The *Purple Sapphire,* superscience, lost races in Central Tibet, survivors of the Great Race. 4 illustrations by Frank R. Paul. v + 532pp.

21180-0 Paperbound $2.50

SEVEN SCIENCE FICTION NOVELS, H. G. Wells. The standard collection of the great novels. Complete, unabridged. *First Men in the Moon, Island of Dr. Moreau, War of the Worlds, Food of the Gods, Invisible Man, Time Machine, In the Days of the Comet.* Not only science fiction fans, but every educated person owes it to himself to read these novels. 1015pp.

20264-X Clothbound $5.00

LAST AND FIRST MEN AND STAR MAKER, TWO SCIENCE FICTION NOVELS, Olaf Stapledon. Greatest future histories in science fiction. In the first, human intelligence is the "hero," through strange paths of evolution, interplanetary invasions, incredible technologies, near extinctions and reemergences. Star Maker describes the quest of a band of star rovers for intelligence itself, through time and space: weird inhuman civilizations, crustacean minds, symbiotic worlds, etc. Complete, unabridged. v + 438pp. 21962-3 Paperbound $2.00

THREE PROPHETIC NOVELS, H. G. WELLS. Stages of a consistently planned future for mankind. *When the Sleeper Wakes*, and *A Story of the Days to Come*, anticipate *Brave New World* and *1984*, in the 21st Century; *The Time Machine*, only complete version in print, shows farther future and the end of mankind. All show Wells's greatest gifts as storyteller and novelist. Edited by E. F. Bleiler. x + 335pp. (USO) 20605-X Paperbound $2.00

THE DEVIL'S DICTIONARY, Ambrose Bierce. America's own Oscar Wilde—Ambrose Bierce—offers his barbed iconoclastic wisdom in over 1,000 definitions hailed by H. L. Mencken as "some of the most gorgeous witticisms in the English language." 145pp. 20487-1 Paperbound $1.25

MAX AND MORITZ, Wilhelm Busch. Great children's classic, father of comic strip, of two bad boys, Max and Moritz. Also Ker and Plunk (Plisch und Plumm), Cat and Mouse, Deceitful Henry, Ice-Peter, The Boy and the Pipe, and five other pieces. Original German, with English translation. Edited by H. Arthur Klein; translations by various hands and H. Arthur Klein. vi + 216pp.
20181-3 Paperbound $1.50

PIGS IS PIGS AND OTHER FAVORITES, Ellis Parker Butler. The title story is one of the best humor short stories, as Mike Flannery obfuscates biology and English. Also included, That Pup of Murchison's, The Great American Pie Company, and Perkins of Portland. 14 illustrations. v + 109pp. 21532-6 Paperbound $1.00

THE PETERKIN PAPERS, Lucretia P. Hale. It takes genius to be as stupidly mad as the Peterkins, as they decide to become wise, celebrate the "Fourth," keep a cow, and otherwise strain the resources of the Lady from Philadelphia. Basic book of American humor. 153 illustrations. 219pp. 20794-3 Paperbound $1.25

PERRAULT'S FAIRY TALES, translated by A. E. Johnson and S. R. Littlewood, with 34 full-page illustrations by Gustave Doré. All the original Perrault stories—Cinderella, Sleeping Beauty, Bluebeard, Little Red Riding Hood, Puss in Boots, Tom Thumb, etc.—with their witty verse morals and the magnificent illustrations of Doré. One of the five or six great books of European fairy tales. viii + 117pp. 8⅛ x 11. 22311-6 Paperbound $2.00

OLD HUNGARIAN FAIRY TALES, Baroness Orczy. Favorites translated and adapted by author of the *Scarlet Pimpernel*. Eight fairy tales include "The Suitors of Princess Fire-Fly," "The Twin Hunchbacks," "Mr. Cuttlefish's Love Story," and "The Enchanted Cat." This little volume of magic and adventure will captivate children as it has for generations. 90 drawings by Montagu Barstow. 96pp.
(USO) 22293-4 Paperbound $1.95

THE RED FAIRY BOOK, Andrew Lang. Lang's color fairy books have long been children's favorites. This volume includes Rapunzel, Jack and the Bean-stalk and 35 other stories, familiar and unfamiliar. 4 plates, 93 illustrations x + 367pp.
21673-X Paperbound $1.95

THE BLUE FAIRY BOOK, Andrew Lang. Lang's tales come from all countries and all times. Here are 37 tales from Grimm, the Arabian Nights, Greek Mythology, and other fascinating sources. 8 plates, 130 illustrations. xi + 390pp.
21437-0 Paperbound $1.95

HOUSEHOLD STORIES BY THE BROTHERS GRIMM. Classic English-language edition of the well-known tales — Rumpelstiltskin, Snow White, Hansel and Gretel, The Twelve Brothers, Faithful John, Rapunzel, Tom Thumb (52 stories in all). Translated into simple, straightforward English by Lucy Crane. Ornamented with headpieces, vignettes, elaborate decorative initials and a dozen full-page illustrations by Walter Crane. x + 269pp.
21080-4 Paperbound $2.00

THE MERRY ADVENTURES OF ROBIN HOOD, Howard Pyle. The finest modern versions of the traditional ballads and tales about the great English outlaw. Howard Pyle's complete prose version, with every word, every illustration of the first edition. Do not confuse this facsimile of the original (1883) with modern editions that change text or illustrations. 23 plates plus many page decorations. xxii + 296pp.
22043-5 Paperbound $2.00

THE STORY OF KING ARTHUR AND HIS KNIGHTS, Howard Pyle. The finest children's version of the life of King Arthur; brilliantly retold by Pyle, with 48 of his most imaginative illustrations. xviii + 313pp. 6⅛ x 9¼.
21445-1 Paperbound $2.00

THE WONDERFUL WIZARD OF OZ, L. Frank Baum. America's finest children's book in facsimile of first edition with all Denslow illustrations in full color. The edition a child should have. Introduction by Martin Gardner. 23 color plates, scores of drawings. iv + 267pp.
20691-2 Paperbound $1.95

THE MARVELOUS LAND OF OZ, L. Frank Baum. The second Oz book, every bit as imaginative as the Wizard. The hero is a boy named Tip, but the Scarecrow and the Tin Woodman are back, as is the Oz magic. 16 color plates, 120 drawings by John R. Neill. 287pp.
20692-0 Paperbound $1.75

THE MAGICAL MONARCH OF MO, L. Frank Baum. Remarkable adventures in a land even stranger than Oz. The best of Baum's books not in the Oz series. 15 color plates and dozens of drawings by Frank Verbeck. xviii + 237pp.
21892-9 Paperbound $2.00

THE BAD CHILD'S BOOK OF BEASTS, MORE BEASTS FOR WORSE CHILDREN, A MORAL ALPHABET, Hilaire Belloc. Three complete humor classics in one volume. Be kind to the frog, and do not call him names . . . and 28 other whimsical animals. Familiar favorites and some not so well known. Illustrated by Basil Blackwell. 156pp.
(USO) 20749-8 Paperbound $1.25

EAST O' THE SUN AND WEST O' THE MOON, George W. Dasent. Considered the best of all translations of these Norwegian folk tales, this collection has been enjoyed by generations of children (and folklorists too). Includes True and Untrue, Why the Sea is Salt, East O' the Sun and West O' the Moon, Why the Bear is Stumpy-Tailed, Boots and the Troll, The Cock and the Hen, Rich Peter the Pedlar, and 52 more. The only edition with all 59 tales. 77 illustrations by Erik Werenskiold and Theodor Kittelsen. xv + 418pp. 22521-6 Paperbound $3.00

GOOPS AND HOW TO BE THEM, Gelett Burgess. Classic of tongue-in-cheek humor, masquerading as etiquette book. 87 verses, twice as many cartoons, show mischievous Goops as they demonstrate to children virtues of table manners, neatness, courtesy, etc. Favorite for generations. viii + 88pp. 6½ x 9¼.
22233-0 Paperbound $1.25

ALICE'S ADVENTURES UNDER GROUND, Lewis Carroll. The first version, quite different from the final *Alice in Wonderland*, printed out by Carroll himself with his own illustrations. Complete facsimile of the "million dollar" manuscript Carroll gave to Alice Liddell in 1864. Introduction by Martin Gardner. viii + 96pp. Title and dedication pages in color. 21482-6 Paperbound $1.25

THE BROWNIES, THEIR BOOK, Palmer Cox. Small as mice, cunning as foxes, exuberant and full of mischief, the Brownies go to the zoo, toy shop, seashore, circus, etc., in 24 verse adventures and 266 illustrations. Long a favorite, since their first appearance in St. Nicholas Magazine. xi + 144pp. 6⅝ x 9¼.
21265-3 Paperbound $1.75

SONGS OF CHILDHOOD, Walter De La Mare. Published (under the pseudonym Walter Ramal) when De La Mare was only 29, this charming collection has long been a favorite children's book. A facsimile of the first edition in paper, the 47 poems capture the simplicity of the nursery rhyme and the ballad, including such lyrics as I Met Eve, Tartary, The Silver Penny. vii + 106pp. 21972-0 Paperbound $1.25

THE COMPLETE NONSENSE OF EDWARD LEAR, Edward Lear. The finest 19th-century humorist-cartoonist in full: all nonsense limericks, zany alphabets, Owl and Pussycat, songs, nonsense botany, and more than 500 illustrations by Lear himself. Edited by Holbrook Jackson. xxix + 287pp. (USO) 20167-8 Paperbound $1.75

BILLY WHISKERS: THE AUTOBIOGRAPHY OF A GOAT, Frances Trego Montgomery. A favorite of children since the early 20th century, here are the escapades of that rambunctious, irresistible and mischievous goat—Billy Whiskers. Much in the spirit of *Peck's Bad Boy*, this is a book that children never tire of reading or hearing. All the original familiar illustrations by W. H. Fry are included: 6 color plates, 18 black and white drawings. 159pp. 22345-0 Paperbound $2.00

MOTHER GOOSE MELODIES. Faithful republication of the fabulously rare Munroe and Francis "copyright 1833" Boston edition—the most important Mother Goose collection, usually referred to as the "original." Familiar rhymes plus many rare ones, with wonderful old woodcut illustrations. Edited by E. F. Bleiler. 128pp. 4½ x 6⅜. 22577-1 Paperbound $1.25

Two Little Savages; Being the Adventures of Two Boys Who Lived as Indians and What They Learned, Ernest Thompson Seton. Great classic of nature and boyhood provides a vast range of woodlore in most palatable form, a genuinely entertaining story. Two farm boys build a teepee in woods and live in it for a month, working out Indian solutions to living problems, star lore, birds and animals, plants, etc. 293 illustrations. vii + 286pp.

20985-7 Paperbound $2.50

Peter Piper's Practical Principles of Plain & Perfect Pronunciation. Alliterative jingles and tongue-twisters of surprising charm, that made their first appearance in America about 1830. Republished in full with the spirited woodcut illustrations from this earliest American edition. 32pp. 4½ x 6⅜.

22560-7 Paperbound $1.00

Science Experiments and Amusements for Children, Charles Vivian. 73 easy experiments, requiring only materials found at home or easily available, such as candles, coins, steel wool, etc.; illustrate basic phenomena like vacuum, simple chemical reaction, etc. All safe. Modern, well-planned. Formerly *Science Games for Children*. 102 photos, numerous drawings. 96pp. 6⅛ x 9¼.

21856-2 Paperbound $1.25

An Introduction to Chess Moves and Tactics Simply Explained, Leonard Barden. Informal intermediate introduction, quite strong in explaining reasons for moves. Covers basic material, tactics, important openings, traps, positional play in middle game, end game. Attempts to isolate patterns and recurrent configurations. Formerly *Chess*. 58 figures. 102pp. (USO) 21210-6 Paperbound $1.25

Lasker's Manual of Chess, Dr. Emanuel Lasker. Lasker was not only one of the five great World Champions, he was also one of the ablest expositors, theorists, and analysts. In many ways, his Manual, permeated with his philosophy of battle, filled with keen insights, is one of the greatest works ever written on chess. Filled with analyzed games by the great players. A single-volume library that will profit almost any chess player, beginner or master. 308 diagrams. xli x 349pp.

20640-8 Paperbound $2.50

The Master Book of Mathematical Recreations, Fred Schuh. In opinion of many the finest work ever prepared on mathematical puzzles, stunts, recreations; exhaustively thorough explanations of mathematics involved, analysis of effects, citation of puzzles and games. Mathematics involved is elementary. Translated by F. Göbel. 194 figures. xxiv + 430pp.

22134-2 Paperbound $3.00

Mathematics, Magic and Mystery, Martin Gardner. Puzzle editor for Scientific American explains mathematics behind various mystifying tricks: card tricks, stage "mind reading," coin and match tricks, counting out games, geometric dissections, etc. Probability sets, theory of numbers clearly explained. Also provides more than 400 tricks, guaranteed to work, that you can do. 135 illustrations. xii + 176pp.

20338-2 Paperbound $1.50

CATALOGUE OF DOVER BOOKS

MATHEMATICAL PUZZLES FOR BEGINNERS AND ENTHUSIASTS, Geoffrey Mott-Smith. 189 puzzles from easy to difficult—involving arithmetic, logic, algebra, properties of digits, probability, etc.—for enjoyment and mental stimulus. Explanation of mathematical principles behind the puzzles. 135 illustrations. viii + 248pp.
20198-8 Paperbound $1.25

PAPER FOLDING FOR BEGINNERS, William D. Murray and Francis J. Rigney. Easiest book on the market, clearest instructions on making interesting, beautiful origami. Sail boats, cups, roosters, frogs that move legs, bonbon boxes, standing birds, etc. 40 projects; more than 275 diagrams and photographs. 94pp.
20713-7 Paperbound $1.00

TRICKS AND GAMES ON THE POOL TABLE, Fred Herrmann. 79 tricks and games—some solitaires, some for two or more players, some competitive games—to entertain you between formal games. Mystifying shots and throws, unusual caroms, tricks involving such props as cork, coins, a hat, etc. Formerly *Fun on the Pool Table*. 77 figures. 95pp.
21814-7 Paperbound $1.00

HAND SHADOWS TO BE THROWN UPON THE WALL: A SERIES OF NOVEL AND AMUSING FIGURES FORMED BY THE HAND, Henry Bursill. Delightful picturebook from great-grandfather's day shows how to make 18 different hand shadows: a bird that flies, duck that quacks, dog that wags his tail, camel, goose, deer, boy, turtle, etc. Only book of its sort. vi + 33pp. 6½ x 9¼. 21779-5 Paperbound $1.00

WHITTLING AND WOODCARVING, E. J. Tangerman. 18th printing of best book on market. "If you can cut a potato you can carve" toys and puzzles, chains, chessmen, caricatures, masks, frames, woodcut blocks, surface patterns, much more. Information on tools, woods, techniques. Also goes into serious wood sculpture from Middle Ages to present, East and West. 464 photos, figures. x + 293pp.
20965-2 Paperbound $2.00

HISTORY OF PHILOSOPHY, Julián Marias. Possibly the clearest, most easily followed, best planned, most useful one-volume history of philosophy on the market; neither skimpy nor overfull. Full details on system of every major philosopher and dozens of less important thinkers from pre-Socratics up to Existentialism and later. Strong on many European figures usually omitted. Has gone through dozens of editions in Europe. 1966 edition, translated by Stanley Appelbaum and Clarence Strowbridge. xviii + 505pp. 21739-6 Paperbound $2.75

YOGA: A SCIENTIFIC EVALUATION, Kovoor T. Behanan. Scientific but non-technical study of physiological results of yoga exercises; done under auspices of Yale U. Relations to Indian thought, to psychoanalysis, etc. 16 photos. xxiii + 270pp.
20505-3 Paperbound $2.50

Prices subject to change without notice.
Available at your book dealer or write for free catalogue to Dept. GI, Dover Publications, Inc., 180 Varick St., N. Y., N. Y. 10014. Dover publishes more than 150 books each year on science, elementary and advanced mathematics, biology, music, art, literary history, social sciences and other areas.